TO WED AT CHRISTMAS

Helen R. Myers

Silhouette
ROMANCE™
Published by Silhouette Books
America's Publisher of Contemporary Romance

For Mary Bracken
Biology Instructor, Bookstore Owner, Gentlest of Scorpios

May all your seasons be bright

 SILHOUETTE BOOKS

ISBN 0-373-19049-2

TO WED AT CHRISTMAS

Copyright © 1994 by Helen R. Myers

This edition published by arrangement with Harlequin Enterprises B.V.

® and TM are trademarks of Harlequin Enterprises B.V., used under license. Trademarks indicated with ® are registered in the United States Patent and Trademark Office, the Canadian Trade Marks Office and in other countries.

Printed in U.S.A.

HELEN R. MYERS

satisfies her preference for a reclusive life-style by living deep in the Piney Woods of East Texas with her husband, Robert, and—because they were there first—the various species of four-legged and winged creatures that wander throughout their ranch. To write has been her lifelong dream, and to bring a slightly different flavor to each book is an ongoing ambition.

Admittedly restless, she sees that as helpful to her writing, explaining, "It makes me reach for new territory and experiment with old boundaries." In 1993, the Romance Writers of America awarded *Navarrone* the prestigious RITA Award for Best Short Contemporary Novel of the Year.

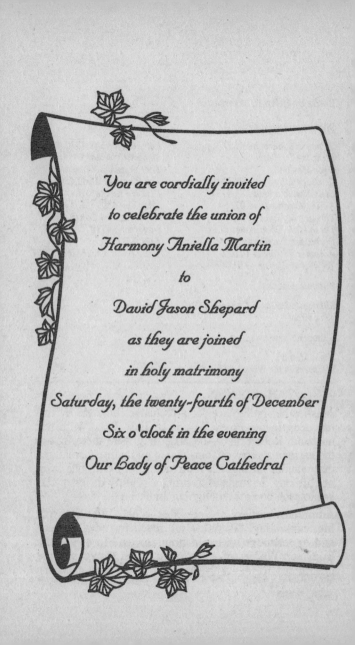

You are cordially invited
to celebrate the union of
Harmony Aniella Martin
to
David Jason Shepard
as they are joined
in holy matrimony
Saturday, the twenty-fourth of December
Six o'clock in the evening
Our Lady of Peace Cathedral

Chapter One

The incident happened the way assaults usually do, quickly and unexpectedly. One moment he was strolling down the sidewalk, surrounded by shoppers, laughter, her music... and he'd been debating over how close he dared get without making her uncomfortable. In the next instant her scream ripped through the night.

Her scream. Oh, yes, he knew the victim immediately, recognized the voice with every atom of his being as easily as he identified the terror in it, even though he was too far away to see what was happening. That was also why, as he launched himself into a dead run down the sidewalk, he had a tougher time fighting the chilling dread that threatened to incapacitate him, or halting the idiotic, inevitable afterthoughts. They came relentlessly, and with a vengeance.

If only I was a half block farther down the street... as good a sprinter as I'd been in school... closer... closer!

God, yes, he wished he'd been closer. But he hadn't wanted to crowd or upset her. It had been enough to be cocooned in the magic of her music, mesmerized by the life she pulled from her instrument.

What if that magic had been stolen from the world forever?

What had happened?

How bad was it?

He charged like a madman, pushing through the pedestrians landscaping downtown Appleton as densely as the trees blanketing the Green Mountains. Too many people, he thought, his anxiety manifesting itself in a pair of hands that threatened to strangle the breath out of him. Far too many for their small Vermont town, even for the beginning of a weekend. But this was no ordinary Friday night; it was the day after Thanksgiving, the start of the holiday shopping season—one of the busiest times of the year.

While unsnapping his holster he thrust his left hand into the air to halt traffic, and raced across Main Street. Tires screeched on the snow-wet pavement, horns blared. Ignoring the commotion, he leapt over the curb and onto the sidewalk, then shouldered his way through another wall of coat-insulated bodies. Each exhaled breath emerged as one long spear of vapor. Even for New England the bitter cold seemed premature, but up until now that had added to the aura of yuletide cheer permeating the streets.

"Police!" he shouted to the human wall thwarting his progress. "Let me through, please. *Move*, people!"

"Did you see them?" someone to his right gasped. "There were two of them. They knocked her backward as if she was a cardboard doll and grabbed the money bucket."

"What are you waiting for?" someone who blocked his way demanded. "Go after those hooligans! We'll take care of her."

It came as no surprise to learn Gladys Silverman had issued that command. Gladys, who owned Secondhand Treasures and often looked as if she was wearing a good portion of her inventory, had a reputation for bossing people around, and although in no mood to be on the receiving end of her lecturing, he knew she was right. Concern for Harmony had slowed him down.

Getting a quick, if sketchy, description from the group, he snapped, "Stay with her, I'll be back!" and went after the assailants as fast as the swarm of curious and concerned onlookers could be made to shuffle out of his way.

As he reported the incident to the station via his portable radio, he covered a two-block area, checking stores, vehicles and especially the shadow-shrouded alleys. Unfortunately, with their considerable head start, the suspects had managed to vanish into the night. Assured by the dispatcher that the rest of the on-duty staff were joining the search, he announced he was returning to Revell's Department Store to see to the victim.

Once there, he found Harmony back on her feet, and most of the crowd dispersed. But his greatest relief came as he realized that her instrument had suffered more damage than she had. The violin's painstakingly cared-for finish now bore a number of ugly scratches, and the bow had been snapped in two. He had a feeling, however, that she wouldn't share his relief or gratitude.

Mrs. Silverman stood shaking her head over the tragedy. "I remember when your grandfather, may he rest in peace, gave that to you. Ernesto Bonifanti...such a talented man, and how proud he'd been that you'd inherited his gift."

Nice going, Mrs. S. Nothing like making her feel worse than she already does. David cleared his throat. "Are you all right, Miss Martin?"

"How do you know my—" she began, spinning around. "Oh!"

He had been expecting this, the look of surprise changing to wariness as she realized who her cavalry had proved to be. He was, after all, a Shepherd and she was a Martin. Not everyone in Appleton knew their story, but most people had at least heard of the deep animosity the Martins felt for the Shepherds.

"Were you injured? Do you need me to call for an ambulance?" He hated feeling tongue-tied like some rookie handling his first incident, rather than a cop completing his third year with the police department. It was her soft brown eyes that tangled him in knots. No, it was more; it was everything about her. She was so damned feminine, and—he didn't care if it was an old-fashioned word—*sweet*. She made him feel awkward and rough around the edges.

"No, no. I'm fine. A bit...rattled, maybe."

"A bit, nothing. She's in shock, Dr. Einstein," Mrs. Silverman snapped on her behalf. The white ostrich feather on her black felt hat bobbed precariously with each animated toss of her head. "You think maybe you can give her the third degree somewhere out of this cold? Come along, Harmony, dear. Let me take you into Revell's. You'll sit down, you'll catch your breath.... Sweetheart!" she cried, clutching the younger woman's hands between hers. "Your fingers are frozen through and through. What were you thinking coming out on a night like this without dressing properly?"

"You can't play the violin wearing gloves, Mrs. Silverman."

Harmony's reply was vague and she continued to stare at David. He noted, however, that her eyes were giving him a different message, something like, *I can't talk to you. You know I can't talk to you. Why do you have to be the one on duty tonight?* Since much the same thing had crossed his mind, if for different reasons, he was relieved Mrs. Silverman had given him a way to escape Harmony's silent reproval, as well as those individuals who lingered in the hope that something exciting might yet occur.

"That's a good idea, Mrs. S. You see that she gets what she needs inside, and I'll join you as soon as I interview a few witnesses out here."

Needing a break from the gut-churning feeling he had whenever his gaze locked with Harmony's, he turned away and announced, "All right, folks, I'll take statements from anyone who had a good look at the suspects."

"Suspects!" Bea Bossman, president of Appleton's beautification committee, huffed from the back of the group. "Did you hear that? Next he'll be calling the perps alleged assailants. Sounds as if your eyesight's as bad as your uncle's was, David Shepherd!"

"Those two were smart fellas, Dave. They were wearing ski masks!" Harvey Teesdale, the town barber, called out.

"Officer Shepherd, I live outside the city limits, do you think it'll be safe to go home?"

"Say they ain't local boys, Davey!"

Except for snooty Mrs. Bossman, David understood the anxiety that lay beneath the passionate outbursts, and that it was part of his job to listen and not take any of it personally. Everyone reacted differently to crime and trauma, and situations like this spawned an adrenaline rush that took time to run its course. Not only was it often healthier to let someone vent and opinionize, but those outbursts sometimes filled in blank spaces in an investigation.

He loved being a cop and had wanted to follow in his father's and uncle's footsteps for as long as he could remember. Not even the tragedy that had traumatized his family all those years ago, nor college and a stint in the service had changed his mind. Some said it was because he took his surname too seriously, that he felt an irrepressible need to give the Shepherds back their reputation as Appleton's most responsible caretakers. If that was the case—and he tried not to dwell on such amateur psychoanalysis—tonight he'd disappointed himself. What's more, any hopes he'd been harboring of getting near Harmony without her siccing the embittered Martin clan on him now looked overambitious, naive at best.

"Okay, let's start from the beginning," he said, drawing out his notebook and pen. "Who, if anyone, saw the assault?"

It took almost twenty minutes before he finished taking statements and could seek out Harmony again.

He discovered that Lawrence Burton, the manager of the department store, had offered the use of his office, and David arrived there to find the victimized schoolteacher surrounded by Larry and Mrs. Silverman. Harmony was actually smiling—until she spotted him in the doorway.

"I'm afraid they got away," he said, aware she'd probably figured that out for herself the moment she'd seen the regret and gloominess that had to be written all over his face.

Larry and Mrs. Silverman exchanged glances, but Harmony simply dropped her gaze to the cup of steaming coffee she held between her still-trembling hands.

"I need to ask her a few questions," he continued, focusing on the two who would make such an event a crowd. "Would you mind stepping outside for a few minutes?"

"No problem." Ever agreeable, Larry patted him on the shoulder. That came as no surprise; they'd known each other for years. Two grades ahead of him in school, Larry had been the football team's star quarterback, a generous-natured soul who'd helped him create his own niche in Appleton High's athletic history. "It'll work out," he offered quietly. "Keep the faith."

Wondering if he'd flunked Poker Face 101, or if Larry had suddenly developed a keen talent for ESP, he replied, "Yeah, sure. Thanks."

Mrs. Silverman proved less accommodating. She lifted shaved and penciled eyebrows that were as black as the fake fur collar on a coat that had seen better days. "I don't know about this. You want me to call your mother, Harmony? I think I should call your mother. No?'' The old woman sighed as Harmony shook her head. "Okay, sweetheart. You know what's best. But if you need anything, I'll be right outside the door.''

"I'm sure I'll be fine, Mrs. Silverman.''

Harmony spoke so softly David had to strain to hear her. It didn't help that his pulse had begun to pound in his ears again. Well, this was the moment he'd been dreaming about for an eternity, and with each second it inched closer. A chance to be alone with her... to speak without eavesdroppers. He almost felt dizzy from the anticipation, until he recalled that if the muggers had been any more brutal, this wouldn't be happening.

And another Shepherd would be condemned to more Martin wrath.

As he heard the door close behind him, David stood in troubled silence trying to decide if he dared take the seat next to her, dared ask outright if she hated him the way the rest of her family did. How many times had he passed her on the street, only to see her look away or detour to avoid him altogether? When it was his turn in a patrol car he punished himself more by driving past the school where she taught junior high music, in the sheer hope of catching a glimpse of her through some window. She always looked so lovely, so fresh. Pure. In a way his thoughts of her weren't. Heaven help him, he had a serious problem when it came to Harmony Martin.

"Are you sure you're all right?'' he began gruffly, combing his hand through his wind-mussed hair. Only recently had his captain stopped trying to force him to wear a hat, after it had become apparent it was too expensive to keep replacing those he'd lost during his dashes to one call or another. His mother still complained, of course, but David shrugged off her concerns for his health with the simple explanation that he was a mover and that was that...in the same way that Harmony had a talent for being incredibly still. "You, um, didn't hurt yourself when you fell?"

"Only my pride." Her smile could be described as wan at best, and she stopped trying to pretend altogether when she looked down at her violin.

Tears were close. David could see that in the tension of her shoulders. If he didn't do something fast, she would soon be breaking down completely. Knowing he wouldn't be able to stand it if she did, he followed his instincts, crouched before her and cupped her hands with his. "We'll get them. I promise you."

The look she gave him said she didn't believe him, and that her lack of faith had nothing to do with how clever the muggers had been. Worse, she gently but decisively inched away from his touch.

David sighed. "Harmony...may I call you Harmony?"

"I still can't believe you know my name."

The statement was made with more concern than surprise. "Just like you know mine," he said, letting her know by his tone he would be disappointed if she tried to pretend otherwise. He knew they'd been aware of each other ever since he was eighteen and she fourteen, the day he and his family had arrived for her father's funeral—and been asked to leave. Twelve years. It seemed like a lifetime.

"My family would be very upset if they knew I was talking to you."

"Sometimes we have to put aside personal differences for the sake of other things," he told her, struggling to remind himself that he had a job to do.

"Couldn't you call in someone else?"

She looked at him with such wrenching appeal that he almost considered it for her sake. Then he gave himself a mental kick.

Just what kind of an excuse will you use with headquarters?

"That's impossible," he said at last, fighting his disappointment. "Foot patrol is my beat tonight and I was the first officer at the scene of the crime. My boss wouldn't care whether you hate me or not. He expects me to do my job."

"I didn't say I—" She bit her lip.

He almost lost his balance as he leaned closer in hope of hearing the rest. "Didn't what?"

"Nothing." She looked at the metal nameplate on Larry's desk, the solid door, the beige, tight-weave carpet that had been picked for utility rather than style...everywhere but at him. "What do you need me to do?"

"Tell me what happened." He reached inside his leather jacket for his pad and pen.

Immediately the wall was back between them, as if he'd asked her for her phone number. "I was mugged!"

He didn't need to be reminded of that. If the beauty of her music had been silenced forever, he would undoubtedly have done something nuts, something that would have stripped him of his badge and gun so fast he might never stop spinning, let alone recover.

"The frustrating part of all this is that there are technicalities that need to be addressed," he said, willing her to listen and to stop running away. "We need to fill out a report for everyone who's a witness and—"

"I know the procedure."

Of course she knew it. Probably almost as well as he did. After all, she'd witnessed the process before, and even though she'd been very young, you never forgot. David sucked in a deep breath. Could he do nothing right?

"I'm sorry."

He'd been thinking the words, but she spoke them. Shifting on the balls of his feet as though she'd tried to pull the carpet from under him, he asked, "*You're* sorry?"

"I'm overreacting."

"Considering what you've been through, you have every right."

"No." She relented and glanced at him from under lashes as dark, as lush as her ebony hair. They almost curled as much, too. "I don't have a right to judge you for something that's not your fault."

Whether she really believed that or not, he felt as if he'd suddenly been catapulted to the summit of a mountain. The air became thin, and he had to fight a wave of dizziness by counting the flashes of gold in her dark brown eyes. "That's very fair of you."

"Please . . . just ask whatever you need to. I have to get back to the Salvation Army station and— Oh, God! The bucket! All that money! There must have been over a hundred dollars in there!"

"I'll replace the money myself." David only realized what he'd said when he saw her expression change to sheer bewilderment. "As for the bucket, it'll probably show up, too."

"Why?"

Bemused, he smiled. "What are they going to do with a red pail? As soon as they get the cash out, they'll toss it. It might need a new coat of paint by then, but—"

"No. That's not what I meant. It's what you said about the donations. Did you mean it?"

"I try not to say anything I don't mean, Harmony."

"But that's a great deal of money."

"Well, I'm not married. I don't have any kids."

She swept back her mane of curls with a hand that continued to tremble from shock. "Yes, but . . . this feels wrong. It isn't your problem and it wouldn't be fair. No, once I explain down at the mission about what happened, they'll understand. Besides, I'm perfectly capable of covering the loss myself."

"And who's going to compensate you for what happened to your violin?"

Once again her lovely eyes lost their inner glow. She reached down and stroked the timeworn case that contained her bruised instrument. "I'm trying not to think about that. I guess you heard that this belonged to my grandfather? He was my mother's father. It's because of him that I learned to play."

David knew all that but let her ramble, hoping it would relieve some of the pressure. He didn't know what he would do if she actually broke down and cried.

"I'll never be as good as he was."

"I'm no expert," he had to interject, "but I think you're pretty terrific."

Again she stared. "You've heard me play?"

He didn't know what fascinated him more, the bottomless depths of those eyes or the invitation created by her soft, parted lips. "Yeah," he managed, certain he sounded more drugged than gravelly.

"I see."

"More than once. I hope that doesn't disturb you?"

It did, though. He could see it in the way she studied him, so solemn and uncertain. Worried, yet intrigued, too. Her curiosity gave him hope. What did she see? he wondered. Was she disappointed? Attracted? It was hard to tell with Harmony Martin.

All his life the female members of his family—and there were enough of them to start a convent or band, since he was the eldest of five children, and *only* son—had been supportive of him, even outrageously prejudiced. They'd told him that he should have been a ski instructor instead of a cop because he was so good-looking. They'd insisted his blond charisma combined with his athletic background were irresistible to women and should be taken advantage of. He enjoyed skiing, had even been good enough to try competing for a while, but he'd always seen himself as a bit too serious to pursue it as a profession, *or* to rely on his looks to get him through life. Did any of that show to someone as real as this gifted young woman?

"I think . . . I think you'd better ask me those questions and I should leave," Harmony whispered, inching back in her chair.

David sighed. He knew he'd made a mistake in letting her see too much of his admiration and attraction. "I didn't mean to embarrass you."

"You haven't."

"Then you're unique in more ways than you know. The mere idea of being watched would disturb most people."

"You didn't," she replied with even less conviction. "But Gladys or someone may call my family. I don't want them to worry."

What she meant was that she didn't want them coming to look for her and demanding answers. David flipped open his notebook. "Of course. Name and—?" He cleared his throat and filled in several of the top lines without her help, aware as she watched in tense silence. Finally he got to a part he didn't know the answer to. "Do you have a description of the men who assaulted you?"

Harmony uttered a sound of disbelief. "Didn't you hear what everyone told you? They were wearing ski masks, and they certainly didn't stop to speak. It all happened so fast I barely realized what was going on until I was lying on the sidewalk!"

David fought a silent war between compassion and duty. "I understand. But the front of the store is fairly well lit."

"Not really. They've substituted decorated wreaths and trees for some of their regular floodlights."

"So you're saying you couldn't identify anything? Not even the color of the ski masks?" He lowered his voice to repress his subtle doubt. "Close your eyes, Harmony. Think about it."

Somewhat reluctantly she did as he instructed. Then a faint frown drew her fine eyebrows together. "Wait. Yes, I do think there was something. One of the masks was solid black. No, blue. It matched his blue jean jacket." Her smile blossomed like his mother's prize roses after a long winter's sleep. "Why—you're right!

I remember thinking that he couldn't be from around here because he wasn't dressed for the cold.''

David couldn't have been more proud of her if she'd given him the man's social security number. "That's good. Now keep going. What about the other one?"

Her smile wilted. "Brown...? Some muddy color with...with a pattern. Maybe. I'm sorry, I can't remember anything about him." She began to turn away to reach for her coat, but a moment later whispered, "Maybe he wore boots? He *did*. Yes...when I fell, he was already running and the headlights from a passing car flashed on the patterned leather!''

"Patterned?"

In her excitement she gestured excitedly. "You know, like cowboys wear."

David's mind raced as he leapt for the phone and punched in 911. The reception would be clearer than his radio and, therefore faster, he decided. After identifying himself, he immediately gave the operator his information and waited for her to pass it on. Less than a minute later she came back on the line and told him that two men fitting the description he'd given her had just been picked up on the other side of town for attempted car theft.

After a few more questions and after assuring headquarters that things were under control, he hung up. "They've got them," he told Harmony, hunkering down before her again. He smiled, foolishly pleased to be the one to pass on the good news. "They were able to get back the money, too. Someone's delivering it to the center right now."

"Oh, that's wonderful!" This time Harmony was the one to reach out. She clasped his hands, and her eyes sparkled with excitement. "Thank you so much."

He began to protest, to tell her that he'd done less than nothing. But caught up in her exuberance, so elated to have her actually talking to him, all he could do was soak in her warmth and happiness like some homeless pup starving for affection.

It didn't take long, though, for her to realize what she was doing. Her smile retreated first. Then she eased her hands from around his, leaving him feeling cold and undeniably empty.

"I . . . I really am grateful," she said at the end of a sigh.

"No more than I am. If you'd been seriously hurt—" his tongue had never felt so thick and clumsy "—I would never have forgiven myself."

As before, she dropped her gaze to the hands she clasped tightly in her lap. Only the deepening color in her cheeks gave away her awareness. "Well, then, I guess that's that. I can go home now?"

"No. Not yet." He spoke on impulse, then struggled to remember the official reason he couldn't let her go. He hoped she was going to be all right with what he had to say. "They're sending a car over to take you to the station. They need you to identify the two men."

She bit her lower lip, moistened it with her tongue. "Does that mean they'll want me to testify in court when the case comes to trial?"

"Probably. That doesn't scare you, does it?"

"A little. Having to face those men again... They'll find out who I am, know where I live. . . ."

"It won't do them any good, Harmony. Those two are going to jail for a long time. If you remember that, it will make testifying much easier."

Nevertheless she continued to look unconvinced. "Will you be there?"

Did he dare hope she wanted him to be? "Probably. The officers involved on a case are usually called in to make an official statement for the court records."

"Then I guess it won't be so scary," she replied, visibly relaxing. "I mean, having someone there who knows what I went through will make it easier."

"Will it?"

She met his probing gaze briefly, then focused on some point on his left shoulder. "I imagine you hear it all the time, but you make me feel...stronger somehow. More confident than I really am."

"That's a strange compliment for a Martin to give a Shepherd."

He told himself he had to be certifiable to bring up *that* subject willingly. But to his surprise, rather than the withdrawal he expected, she looked sad, almost regretful.

"My family may still harbor ill feelings because of what happened back then, but...I don't feel it should affect my gratitude for what you did for me tonight. I think...I think you're a very good Shepherd," she murmured, smiling as if she'd only then realized she'd made the gentle pun.

David made a pretense of groaning, although inside he nearly burst from pleasure. "Have mercy, woman! Do you know how many times I've had to listen to jokes about my name? In the service they even nicknamed me "Pilgrim" because I was always helping the weaker and slower guys in our company."

Harmony nodded as if she already suspected this. "You know, I remember seeing you in your air force uniform when you came home for Christmas one year. You turned all the girls' heads in church.''

"Yours, too?" He figured it would be a waste of energy to try to disguise his hope as something else.

For a moment she looked as though she might confirm that wish, but suddenly she bowed her head and said, "Do you think the squad car has arrived yet?"

Disappointed, but telling himself that she'd been kinder to him than he'd had reason to expect, he rose. "I'll go see. I, ah, I wish I could take you over to the station myself, but I'm still on duty. In fact, I should already be back out on the street." That was the mayor's demand after the most recent upswing of crime in the surrounding counties, a situation they all hoped was temporary, one of the negative aspects of the holidays. Let the citizens see the uniforms, was the theory, and David had been happy to comply—until Harmony had come into the picture.

"Please don't get into trouble because of me."

As she jumped from the chair and reached for her coat, he hurried to assist her. The hyacinth scent that rose from her hair was an unexpected bonus, as was the way the blue wool of her coat brought out the highlights in her curls. With unrepentant pleasure he drew it deep, filing away, too, how they seemed to be made for each other—she just reached his chin, he gauged before she picked up her violin case.

She clutched the cherished item to her as if it were a child. "Thank you again...Officer Shepherd."

David couldn't quite keep from wincing at her formal tone; after all, it wasn't as if she didn't know his first name. "Couldn't you try calling me David?"

"David."

She barely whispered it and yet he felt the sound through his entire body, wondered if it could possibly feel better, and knew it could—uttered against his lips. Then she broke the spell by starting for the door.

He reached out and touched her sleeve. "Harmony." She froze…cast him a curious but wary look, and he sighed. "Can I ask you something?"

She knew what was coming, he could tell. Fear made her eyes go wide and almost opaque, like a stalked deer's.

"I don't think that would be a good idea."

"Why not?"

"You know why." Her grip tightened around her case. "If my family finds out I've been talking to you, they're going to be terribly upset."

"We've done nothing wrong. You needed help. I'm a cop."

"The wrong one."

Images of the past, the unexpected pounding at the door that night twelve years ago, the disjointed, but distinguishably strained voice of his uncle, the word *dead* coming through like the bullet that had killed Harmony's father…it all flashed before David's eyes again, just as it had a thousand times since the night her family's life, along with his, had turned inside out. He blinked the visions away because he'd waited too long for this moment to let it slip through his fingers.

"You don't believe that." He wanted to force her to look at him, but knew the biggest mistake right now would be to touch her. He watched her profile as she swallowed. It stirred his guilt again for taking advantage of her in a weak moment, but not enough to offset the pulsating urgency in him to hear her honest reply. "Tell me, Harmony. Do you think I'm the wrong man?"

"I'm trying not to."

"Then why can't I ask my question?"

"Because this is crazy."

"Maybe. But who knows if I'm ever going to get the chance to ask it again?"

"David, please."

"No." Cautiously reaching out, he touched her hair to prove to himself that she was more than a dream. "I have to do this. I'm going to ask what I've been meaning to for a long time. Harmony Martin... would you go out with me?"

Chapter Two

Harmony thought her lungs would burst from holding her breath for so long. Then again, she told herself as she stood in frozen limbo, she should be getting used to it; after all, she'd been doing little else since she'd realized *he* was the policeman who'd come to her aid. And could she really pretend to be surprised that David Shepherd had asked her out? No, if there was an ounce of honesty in her, she had to admit she'd been expecting this for some time. Fearing it. The question was, why hadn't she run away? But even as she asked herself that, she knew the answer.

It wouldn't have been fair. It wouldn't have been right.

As she exhaled and drew in a much-needed fresh breath, she knew she had to edit that thought. She hadn't run because it wouldn't have resolved anything. And because one of the biggest moments in her life had remained, in a way, unresolved, she was tenacious about keeping her life organized and uncomplicated. Therefore, something had to be done about this situation, this...strange awareness between them. Regardless of the poor timing, she had to acknowledge it so she could ask him to help her put an end to it.

"You know I can't go out with you," she began carefully, wanting above all not to be cruel. "What you're asking would only cause too many people stress and—"

"This has nothing to do with them," David interjected with the quiet confidence that had impressed her for longer than he could know. "This is about you and me."

You and me.

The phrase sent a tingling current straight through her, and left her ashamed for enjoying the delicious warmth that lingered. She'd been trying to convince herself for ages that her attraction to David Shepherd was one-sided; it was how she'd coped with the guilt. His disclosure that she'd been wrong, that he, too, recognized something, proved as distressing as it was exciting. Maybe there was some viability to the theory that most people developed a crush or two in their lives that was hard to explain, but she was twenty-six, for heaven's sake, and he was...

He was David Shepherd. *Shepherd.* A man whose name epitomized all the pain, bitterness and hatred her family had lived with for the past dozen years.

Twelve years ago David's uncle, Douglas Shepherd, had also been a member of the Appleton police force, and one night shortly after Thanksgiving he'd answered a burglary call at Martin's Nursery, Harmony's father's place of business. Except for spring, the holiday season had been William Martin's busiest time of year. He'd often worked late to fill flocked Christmas tree orders, and to bind more pine branches together for the living garland that was so popular to string over mantels and around stairway balustrades. People for miles around had known of his dedication to fill orders as quickly as possible, and someone had taken advantage of that commitment.

But it hadn't been the armed robber who'd prematurely ended William Martin's life. Her father had been shot and killed by Officer Douglas Shepherd. David's uncle. No one, from her mother and three brothers, to Grandmother Irena, who had already been living with them, had yet managed to reconcile themselves to that tragedy.

How could David ask her to forget all that?

How had she let herself become infatuated with the nephew of her father's murderer?

"I can't do this." Once again she bolted for the door. "I'm very grateful for all you've done. I'll tell them down at the station that you were extremely thorough and helpful. But—"

"I'd rather you tell me what I have to do to make you stop treating me as if I were a monster."

David's quiet statement put an abrupt end to her nervous chatter. But she stayed facing the door. "I don't do that."

"Almost. You're afraid of me."

She was afraid of what he made her feel, what he made her yearn for. Ever since her father's death— well, she'd been numb with shock at the funeral and didn't remember much of that, but in the weeks and months and years after—she'd known when David would look at her. His gray eyes would turn apologetic, his young, strongly molded face, so wise even then, would lose the smile he had for everyone else. There had always been something different about him, and somehow that had separated him from the rest of his family. Her older brother, Rod, had rebuked her whenever he'd caught her covertly studying David, but she'd continued feeling a need to figure out who this Shepherd was. She still hadn't succeeded.

"I feel as if I'm caught between a nightmare and a fairy tale," she whispered, trying to make him understand. "And my life is too complicated for fairy tales."

But when she reached for the doorknob, David covered her hand with his. "Harmony, please!"

She froze, stared at that union. His hand was big and sturdy, his skin so much darker than hers from being out in the weather at all hours and seasons. In contrast, she was an indoors person; not because she didn't enjoy nature, gardening and fresh air, but her first love was music, and between it and her teaching responsibilities, her time for other pleasures was limited. Seeing those differences gave her a visual appreciation of just how unsuitable it was for any contact between them.

"Let me go, David."

"I know my timing's bad."

"Not bad. Impossible." She couldn't say more, let alone think, with him so close, touching her. "Please, let me leave."

Somehow she got outside, practically toppling Mrs. Silverman in the process. The older woman grabbed her arm and looked hard into what she imagined was her dazed face.

"What's wrong? Did he get rough with you?"

Rough? As impressively strong as he was physically, she'd never thought of David as being capable of being hard or violent with a woman, and the last thing she wanted was for someone to get the wrong idea, to get him into trouble. "No. It's me. I guess I'm more shaken by all this than I'd thought."

She considered the woman, whom she barely knew save for exchanging a few words whenever their paths crossed. Harmony's impression of Gladys was that beneath the eccentric appearance and odd clothes was a caring soul. She'd proved it tonight. "Mrs. Silverman, would it be an inconvenience to ask if you'd come with me to the station? They want me to identify the men they've arrested."

"Of course I'm coming with you," her self-appointed guardian angel replied with a wave to dismiss the question. "Your mother would want you to have another woman around even if it is a near stranger. And I'll call *her* as soon as we get to the station in case some busybody has already telephoned her and given her a fright. Everything's going to be fine, sweetheart. You'll see."

Grateful though she was, Harmony didn't believe that. She knew as long as she could recall the sensations of David's touch, nothing would ever be all right again.

The extroverted shopkeeper was, however, as good as her word. She accompanied Harmony to the police station chauffeured by a less familiar, portly officer named Platt. Seemingly enjoying the opportunity to ride in the back seat of a police car, Gladys Silverman chattered away.

"If I'd known I was going to the police station tonight, I would have worn my good leather gloves. You know, the street decorations look rather odd when you're viewing them from behind steel mesh. Do you suppose Officer Platt would turn on his lights if we asked him?"

The whimsical monologue almost had Harmony smiling by the time they were pulling in to the station's private parking lot.

"Lucky for you young Shepherd showed when he did," Gladys declared with a satisfied sigh.

Unprepared for that one, Harmony didn't quite know how to respond. "You think so?"

"Of course! He's young, strong.... If those two hooligans had hung around, David would have been able to handle them single-handed. He's what they used to call virile in my day."

Harmony thought that in Mrs. Silverman's day young men wouldn't dare speak to a girl the way David had spoken to her, let alone touched her. But the older woman was right about his being virile. That tiny bit of reflection saved her from slipping into total terror at the thought of having to go into the station, and she sent the woman an appreciative smile.

How on earth had this strange little woman ended up in Appleton? Vermont people were hardly exotic. There was a common denominator that ran through them not unlike the saltiness the citizens of Maine were known for, and the sturdiness those from the plains states were reported to exude. Somewhere in between were the residents of Vermont... stalwart and proud in their own right, and friendly enough in a polite sort of way, but conservative. Gladys Silverman stuck out the way a flamingo would in a chicken coop.

All she knew through hearsay was that the woman had been a child survivor of World War II Europe, where most of her family had been lost. Harmony supposed that was why she radiated a unique zest for living, and why she had a reputation for being unapologetically outspoken.

She decided she liked Gladys Silverman, and made herself a promise that in gratitude she would visit Secondhand Treasures in the near future. After listening to a few ladies at church, Gran Irena insisted there was nothing in the dark, side-street shop that would interest them, but her grandmother could be a bit of an elitist at times.

Thinking of that, Harmony hooked her arm through the old woman's as they walked up the sidewalk together and began, "You know, Mrs. Silverman, I'd better make that call to my family. They're going to be shaken by the news and it will reassure them to hear my voice."

Officer Platt shuffled before them and quickly pulled open the glass door that currently was adorned with a huge red vinyl bow. Gladys Silverman beamed at him and fluttered what Harmony considered the most incredible false eyelashes she'd ever seen.

Once they passed the policeman, the woman whispered to her conspiratorially, "I understand completely, darling. You have nothing to fear from me. I may have a reputation for being a big mouth, but I do know when to keep it shut."

Grateful, Harmony gave her an affectionate squeeze. "Thank you. I think you're a dear lady."

That earned her a disappointed, slightly sour look. "To tell you the truth, sweetie, I'd rather be outrageous, but for you I'm willing to make an exception."

* * *

An hour later and numbed by the countless number of people who'd interviewed her, Harmony signed the various forms shoved before her and decided she was ready to let Mrs. Silverman be outrageous and do whatever was necessary to break her out of this place. Through the whole episode the ruddy-cheeked woman had stayed close, patting her and being reassuring whenever an officer left the conference room to either get another form or check on the status of the muggers, who were being processed somewhere in the back of the station.

Finally she signed her statement and was able to walk out of the room with Mrs. Silverman. There she found Rod waiting for her.

Like David, her oldest brother was thirty, but unlike the man who kept invading her thoughts, he was barely inches taller than her own five foot five. They had both inherited most of their looks from the maternal side of the family, their mother's dark Italian features. Rod, however, also had her rich olive complexion, while Harmony had inherited their father's fair Anglo skin. As he ran a hand through his collar-length black hair, a gesture that made his stark, sharp features more pronounced, she rushed across the hall and hugged him for a long, emotion-filled minute.

"Hell, kid," he finally muttered.

She hugged him tight, grateful for the love she felt emanating from him. "Watch it, mister. Just because Mama's not around doesn't mean you're allowed to swear."

"You think this is swearing? You should have heard me driving down here after your call. You scared the heck out of me, you know?"

"I'm sorry to drag you out at this hour. You probably just got home from the nursery, didn't you?"

As soon as he'd turned twenty-one Rod had taken over the full-time running of the family business, to allow their exhausted mother to work only on weekends and spend more time with the twins, who were now fourteen and high school freshmen. Harmony understood what kind of a toll that took on Rod's private life. Like her, he'd sacrificed to help support the family, and as a result he barely had one. Thinking about his most promising period when he'd been interested in her friend Paula, she knew they'd all taken him for granted too long.

"Don't you worry about me," he muttered, scowling at her. "The guys up front told me their version of what happened. Sounds like you're the one who needs coddling."

This was a familiar routine with him. Whenever something went wrong at the store, or a surprise dentist or household bill came up that would add pressure to the family's comfortable but modest budget, he was always the first to say, "Don't worry about it" or "I'll take care of it." Maybe this attack on top of their violent past was making her overly sensitive or protective of her loved ones, but Harmony thought things needed to change. Rod needed some relief from too much responsibility.

She leaned back to study him, and gave him a gentle shake. "You need to let me thank you, Rod. You need to admit if you're tired, and that in its own way this is as much a strain on you as it is on me."

He eyed her skeptically, his heavy brows nearly meeting in the middle of his forehead. "Did you hit your head on the sidewalk when you fell?"

She understood his reaction. Martins didn't complain about their plight in life, just as they rarely went to the doctor, or accepted charity. They believed in keeping a stiff upper lip, as firmly as they believed hot tea with honey and a spritz of lemon was all that was necessary if a cold was trying to set in. But while she agreed that ancient gastronomical remedies held their own merit, as did the right mental attitude, everything had its exceptions and this moment was one of them.

"No, you stubborn man. I may have a black-and-blue elbow, but that's about it. I just thought it was time we stopped pretending to each other that everything's always perfect. My goodness, looking for the positive in things is important, I know, but if you ask me, this family carries it to the extreme. I think the whole lot of us is suffering from a bad case of denial."

He nodded after every few words that gushed out of her, but when she finished, he simply patted her shoulder awkwardly. "That's it. We're outta here. Good thing tomorrow is Saturday and you get to sleep late, otherwise Mom and Gran would insist you call in sick."

Harmony choked back a sound of frustration. How exasperating to be treated as if she were a ten-year-old with a concussion. Then again, she mused, maybe she had an injury. A concussion of the heart.

With a weary smile she linked her arm through his. "All right, I'll go quietly, oh, wise one. For now. But we do need to talk soon. Really talk."

"Whatever you say, kid. Let's just get out of this place. It gives me the creeps."

What it did was remind him of the past, and because she understood, and felt the same way, Harmony wasn't about to protest—except for one thing. "Wait a minute. Mrs. Silverman?"

The old woman was conversing with a female officer. Harmony led Rod over to them. Offering a polite smile to the woman, who looked almost her age, Harmony said to her guardian angel, "This is my brother, Rod. Rod, this is Mrs. Silverman. She's been holding my hand through this. Could we give her a lift home?"

"We'll take her, Miss Martin," the officer interjected. "You make sure you get home and get some rest."

"For once I agree with you people," Rod said, nodding to Mrs. Silverman. "Let's go, sis."

"Rod." Although she didn't fight him as he hurried her to the exit, she couldn't ignore his behavior, or that he'd sounded as though he rated female officers as low as he did the male members of the force. "I know we're both uncomfortable in here, but that's no justification for being rude."

Instead of answering her, he muttered, "Well, well. Here comes another good soldier now. Hello, Shepherd. Too bad someone else wasn't on duty when my sister was mugged. Maybe then her attackers would have been caught sooner and she wouldn't have had to spend so much time in here being reminded why she shouldn't rely on cops."

"Stop it!" she whispered, squeezing her brother's arm in rebuke. But her look of appeal and regret was all for David, who'd stopped at the doorway. She had no idea why he was back at the station, but he looked cold, and as tired as she felt.

To her relief, the dislike flickering in his eyes died when he met her gaze. What replaced it reminded her that although she'd gone out with several people since she'd started dating, it was only the occasional glances she'd intercepted from him that made her heart beat uncontrollably.

She hoped he might play it safe and smart and let them pass. Instead, he continued to block their way.

"Is everything all right?" he asked her. His tone was low, tender, and as intimate as a brush of his fingers against her cheek.

"Yes, thank you, David. They said I'm finished. Well, at least until the trial. I have to admit I'm not looking forward to that."

He nodded, his expression turning sympathetic. "You'll do fine. But if there's anything you need—"

"She doesn't need anything from you, Shepherd," Rod snapped. "She has her family."

"Rod, please. David was only—" Harmony could feel her brother's tension. Even the arm around her waist tightened with warning, and before she could finish, he urged her past David.

"C'mon. I have to get out of here before I get sick."

Deciding the faster they left, the better, Harmony let her brother move her away. Only when she felt the wind rushing through the entryway tug her scarf from around her neck did she glance back again. She saw David catch it before it fluttered to the ground.

She could have called out for Rod to stop so she could get it back. So could David. But neither of them did. As the door thumped shut behind them Harmony wondered about that, about her sanity.

"David?" Rod marched her to the green pickup with the white logo announcing Martin's Nursery on the door. "*David!* Harry, have you lost your mind?"

He'd christened her with the nickname as a child, back when saying "Harmony" had been a mouthful. Somehow the habit had never worn off, despite the fact that their mother and grandmother despised it for its lack of femininity. Harmony adored it, as she did Rod, but he had to understand that there came a time when she might want to test new things, while retaining those beloved old traditions. "Rod, don't be unfair. He was wonderful to me."

"Didn't you hear me back in there? If he'd been doing his job, this wouldn't have happened."

"He *was* doing his job, and if you could have seen how packed the streets and sidewalks were, you would have been impressed with how quickly he reached me."

As soon as she was seated, Rod slammed the truck door. Circling the front and sliding in on the driver's side, he demanded, "I can't believe you're defending him."

"It has nothing to do with defending, it has to do with being fair. David did his job, Rod. Good heavens, what else could anyone ask of the man?"

Her brother's sturdy chin jutted as he started the truck's engine. "I know what I wish. I wish he didn't exist."

Harmony stared, horrified. "You can't mean that!"

"Why not? He represents everything we've lost," he retorted, his indignation evident as he brutally started the engine.

"It's unfair. Please don't ever say anything so terrible in my presence again."

They drove several blocks in silence, and not even the garland-decorated streetlights, the picture-framed shop windows, or the gaily decorated homes could ease the tension in Harmony. She was glad when they turned down their street.

Their house wasn't far from downtown, and the two-story brick structure stood in one of the older but respectable parts of the community. Since this was the first year that financial pressures weren't a monthly dilemma, they'd indulged in a little decorating, too. Blue multistemmed candles lit every window, and the front door's wreath was adorned with blue and silver balls, which a blue floodlight illuminated.

Something about the serene view must have touched Rod as much as it did her because as they pulled in to their street he said with decided weariness, "I'm not trying to make you as bitter as me, Harry. You have the soft heart in the family, and in a way we all appreciate that. Need it, too. But *you* need to understand that appreciation has its limits. Shepherd is it for me. I'll bet the rest of the family would say the same thing."

Harmony knew he was right. Nevertheless, she felt compelled to reply, "It was inevitable that someone in the family would have contact with a Shepherd eventually, Rod. Appleton isn't big enough to avoid it forever. What's more, I think you're blowing this way out of proportion. Being polite doesn't mean you've surrendered your principles."

"I don't like him," Rod replied, pulling in to their driveway. He parked so that she could walk straight up the sidewalk to the house, then shut off the engine. "What's more, I don't want him anywhere near you. He looks at you funny."

Of course he'd seen David's heated glance. She'd been foolish to hope he hadn't. And knowing her brother would hit the roof if she replied that her reaction to David was mutual, she let the subject drop.

Almost immediately she remembered something she would never have believed she could forget. "My car! Rod—my car's still in town!"

"So? You don't need to worry about it now. We can pick it up sometime tomorrow."

As she climbed out of the truck, Rod followed carrying her violin. She was amazed at how bad she did feel; her muscles and joints were sore and stiffening more with every minute. If this was what football players complained about after a game, maybe she owed them an apology for thinking they had the cushiest jobs.

Midway up the walk the door was thrust open and her mother stepped onto the front porch to greet them. Behind her, peering through the storm door, was Gran Irena.

"Oh, Harmony...my girl...my angel."

Topping the stairs, Harmony felt tears choke her as she moved into her mother's arms. As always, she was struck again at how amazing it was that this tiny woman had given birth to twins. Except for the amount of gray in her mother's hair, they could have been sisters—and her mother was the smaller, more slender one. She had, however, the strength of someone twice her size.

"I'm fine, Mama. Everything's okay."

"When we got the news, my heart stopped. I don't know what I would have done if I'd lost you, too," the older woman sobbed.

Summoning a beaming smile for her grandmother, who was watching the exchange through teary eyes, she replied, "But it didn't. Now let's all go inside before you catch pneumonia."

Once through the front door she was not only engulfed in her grandmother's arms, but the twins made a rare appearance, descending from the cavern of their bedroom. The noise level was almost as overwhelming as the cold had been, and Harmony was grateful when Gran Irena scolded them on everyone's behalf.

"Boys—boys! *Per favore.* So much noise. *Questo non va.* This is not working. Shut off the machine or I take a broom to your backsides. *Bravissimo,*" she said, when they obligingly tuned down their portable stereo.

"Hey, sis," Christopher asked, looking more wide-eyed and unsure than she'd seen him since he was a baby, "are you really okay?"

"Sure." She winked at the teenager who, like his brother, shared their Latin coloring but was far taller than the rest of the family. "And I have an idea—let's go to the kitchen and make hot chocolate. Then we can warm up and I'll tell you all about it."

Always claiming to be starving, Brandon heartily agreed and asked if that meant they could have another cannoli. Wanting to keep the happy atmosphere, and aware that Rod remained somewhat back from the group, Harmony announced she would like a pastry, too.

"You hear that, Olivia?" her grandmother Irena gasped as though reading a cue card. "Miss Chicken Legs herself says she's hungry. Now if that doesn't convince you that she's all right, nothing will."

As they trekked down the hallway of the big old house, and Harmony breathed in the wonderful aroma of spices and the pine they used in abundance to decorate, she glanced at Rod and found him looking anything but fooled.

"You going to tell them everything?" he murmured, stretching to hold the door open for her as they brought up the end of the parade.

"I have nothing to hide," she whispered back. "And I wish you'd stop looking at me as if I did."

"That's guilt talking and you know it." He forced her to pause a moment and said into her ear, "Be careful, Harry. It would kill Mom and Gran if you did something foolish."

As embarrassed as she was annoyed, Harmony walked away from him and forced a smile for the rest of her family. But despite trying to convince herself that she had no reason to feel guilty, she did.

Watching her mother and grandmother bustle around the kitchen with graceful economy, and her brothers devour not one but two Italian pastries apiece while elbowing and teasing each other, she was soothed by a sense of warmth and love. How lucky she was. Yes, they'd lost her father, and they'd survived some tough times. But they'd made it, and were stronger for their experiences. Any contact she had in the future with David Shepherd would only undermine that growth. She couldn't do that to them.

And yet she also couldn't forget the way David had hovered over her, so attentive and caring. Didn't she have a right to have a man look at her the way he had? To feel the things he'd made her feel? To go out with whomever she chose and laugh, dream, enjoy life?

"Dear? Are you sure you're all right?"

Her mother's concerned voice seemed like a cashmere shawl and Harmony wished she could wrap herself up in it and sleep for a week. Maybe then this situation would be reduced to only a memory and looming decisions wouldn't seem quite so overwhelming.

"Tell us what happened," her grandmother coaxed, also watching with concern from her post at the stove. "It will make you feel better. Then you can put it behind you."

"Yeah," Chris urged, a white ring of cream circling his mouth. "Did you get to belt those guys for knocking you on your duff?"

"Christopher Michael Martin!" their mother chided sharply.

"It's all right, Mama." In truth Harmony was glad to be denied too much time for introspection. "Now that it's over I can see the episode had its funny moments...and no, spaghetti legs," she added to the older twin, "I didn't even see the men. I only had to describe their clothing and give the police my statement." Her expression turned somber for a moment as she glanced at her grandmother. "They knocked Gramps's violin out of my hand, Gran. It's scratched badly and the bow snapped. I'm sorry."

"You think we'd be happier if it was in perfect condition and *you* were worse for wear?" her grandmother retorted, ever the pragmatist. "Now stop keeping us in suspense. Tell us everything."

With a loving smile for the woman who had taught her enough Italian to make music theory and various other classes less traumatic, along with the art of pastry making and how to make a five-year-old dress look almost new, she drew in a deep breath and began reciting her story.

It wasn't so difficult. As a teacher, she knew how to perform for an audience, how to capsulize, how to edit—in this case not for time, but for her audience's feelings.

But inevitably they had to be told who the police officer on the scene had been, and she said it as dispassionately as possible, avoiding Rod's quiet gaze from the head of the table. Her mother was the first to react.

"You poor darling," she murmured, putting Harmony's mug of rich, steaming chocolate before her. "That must have been a terrible strain on you."

"Well, I did feel somewhat off balance at first, but..."

"Off balance?" Her grandmother sniffed with a disdain that no one else she'd ever known had managed to mimic. Like her daughter, Irena Bonifanti had a swanlike, graceful neck and a lush mane of hair that, though gray, she'd rarely cut. She kept it neat by coiling it at her nape. "It's a wonder you survived the ordeal with only a few bruises. Those Shepherds are forever throwing their weight around. Just the other day their youngest girl was making a scene in the supermarket over some boy who worked there. It was a disgrace."

Harmony had no way to prove or disprove that statement, and understood that dating had changed significantly since her grandmother and even her mother had been single. But her family didn't waste energy on rationalizations like that when it came to the

Shepherds. As far as she was concerned, however, the Shepherd girls—all four of them—were pretty, intelligent girls with fine manners and a zest for living. She'd had the youngest in her music class for one semester and had rather admired Shawna's spunk, if not her irreverent sense of humor.

"Officer Shepherd was courteous and conscientious," she said, although she knew her family didn't want to hear that. "But I didn't really spend much time with him. Another officer drove me to the station and then I spoke with a constant stream of people." Seeing Rod's jaw flex, she sighed inwardly and decided she wasn't up to parrying any more tonight. "You know, on second thought, I would really like to soak in a hot tub."

"Good idea!" Her mother sprang to her side and helped her scoot back her chair. "You go on up, dear. Take your cocoa. Make sure the water's extra hot to get the soreness out of your muscles. I'll come with you and turn down your bed. Mama, maybe you should set some water on for a hot-water bottle. Boys, if you two inhale one more of those cannoli, I'll report you to your wrestling coach."

Brandon croaked, "He'll bench us, Mom!"

"He'll make us run laps until we're down to our competition weight," Christopher groaned, dropping his head in his hands.

They made it easy for Harmony to find a smile as she withdrew. But as she eased around the table, she was aware of Rod frowning at her. Uh-oh, she thought. *Whatever it is, don't . . . please don't.*

"Harmony?" he murmured just before she made it through the doorway. "I've only just noticed, but what happened to the scarf you always wear when you're playing? You know, the one that was Mom's? I thought you had it when I picked you up at the station."

Chapter Three

She was remarkable.

With the strains of "Oh, Little Town of Bethlehem" floating at him from across the street, David slipped his hand inside his jacket to feel the scarf he wanted to protect from the evening's falling snow. After snatching up the length of silk yesterday when Harmony's brother had rushed her out of the station, he'd thought it too good to be true that she hadn't retraced her steps and asked for it back. Now as he took his break and finished the cup of coffee he'd picked up at the café behind him, he was enjoying yet another treat—the gift of listening to her play.

Just like yesterday she was posted outside Revell's. Apparently she'd found another bow for her instrument, and the violin itself must not have been as badly damaged as he'd thought. But what really amazed him was that she had come out at all.

Yesterday she'd experienced the kind of shock that would have devastated some grown men he knew. Anything could have happened . . . she could be in a hospital at this moment fighting for her life. Nevertheless, there she stood, looking pale and chilled to be sure, but also brave and, dear heaven, so lovely. Clearly she was determined not to be thwarted by last night's experience.

David's chest swelled with gratitude and pride. He knew he had no right to hold such a depth of feeling for this woman when they were barely on speaking terms. But he couldn't deny the feelings existed, either. Nor could he pretend that this was exactly where he had hoped she would be tonight. A woman who frightened easily, who cowered in the face of adversity and life's challenges wouldn't be up to what he wanted, needed of her. And despite her responses yesterday, he had hope in his heart for that future. In fact, as she ended the song and thanked the couple who dropped a bill into her Salvation Army pot, he saw opportunity begin to unfold before him.

She, too, had decided to take a break. With her violin in her left hand, she unhooked the donation pot with her right and retreated into the glass-enclosed foyer of the department store to warm herself. David knew he didn't have a prayer for complete privacy with her, and he also didn't have much time left on *his* break. While this wasn't the perfect scenario by any stretch of the imagination, the softly lit foyer would do. With the determination of a man on a mission, he tossed his empty cup into a trash bin on the corner and hurried across the street.

"Busy watching your flock, Shepherd?" one of the local merchants called as they passed midway across the intersection.

"Something like that, Mr. Theodore. Be careful near the curbs, the slush is starting to refreeze and it's getting slippery."

He didn't mind that people often teased him about his name, or his attentiveness. Even his mother had often suggested that he should have been born a girl and his sisters should have been boys because he was far more the caretaker type than they were. Nodding at a few more townspeople, and winking at two teenage girls who passed him with wistfulness and invitation in their young eyes, he all but leapt onto the sidewalk, his own excitement difficult to contain.

She stood in the most private corner of the enclosed entryway, the left one where, on the other side of the polished pane, shrubbery decorated with tiny white lights blinked merrily. It almost kept time to the piped-in Christmas music coming from the overhead speakers. His heart clenched when Harmony spotted him and he saw the complicated look of pleasure and anxiety that crossed her face.

He closed the few yards between them. "Don't be afraid," he said, keeping his voice low. "I'm not going to cause a scene."

"You shouldn't be here."

She'd replied in kind, her gaze darting to see if anyone was watching. But she needn't have worried; the people who passed were either preoccupied, tired or in a hurry. Few gave them a first, let alone a second look.

Exhaling with relief, Harmony added, "But I knew you would come."

"I had to see how you were."

"I'm fine. Thank you for asking."

"You look more than fine. You look lovely." She wore a different coat tonight, no doubt because her other one had to be sent to the cleaners. This one, actually a long jacket in an electric blue, brought out the sheen in her raven black hair and accented the translucency of her skin. Unable to stop himself, he gently brushed a few lingering snowflakes from the top curls. "But you really shouldn't be out here again so soon."

"That's what my mother said. Unfortunately, they're shorthanded at the center, and this snow is worrisome for some of the older volunteers. It keeps them from fulfilling their scheduled hours. I couldn't add to the dilemma."

"No, never you." He savored the rush of tenderness that warmed him. "That's why I've been staying close."

"You expect more trouble?"

He could have kicked himself for obliterating the light in her eyes, and quickly shook his head. "The men who attacked you are locked away. However, we can't forget that there's plenty more wherever they came from. There always are, Harmony. We have to adjust to offset their threat over us. But the bottom line is that I don't intend to let anything happen to you again."

She lowered her eyes, which added to a natural demureness that compounded her femininity. "You've been very good to me. I'm sorry that Rod didn't see that."

"You don't need to apologize. It's enough to know you don't share his bitterness." With that David reached into his jacket and brought out her scarf. "I also wanted a chance to return this."

To him the scarf was one of a kind, like her—black silk with swirls of red streaking through it. Understated but elegant . . . and he'd added a touch more. Handing her carefully folded possession to her, he saw her eyes widen at the filigree gold butterfly pin he'd found at Gladys Silverman's earlier today.

"David . . . I can't accept this."

"You don't like it?"

She looked as if he'd just asked if she had something against sunsets, moonbeams and rainbows. "How could I not like it? It's . . . Oh, dear. I cringe when I hear people use the word *precious*, but this is. Precious." She traced the delicate, complicated threading that made up the wings. Then the gemstones making up the eyes that were unmistakably sapphires. She bit her lower lip. "It's simply too much."

"Not as far as I'm concerned."

Once again she looked overwhelmed, torn. "Last night Rod asked me about the scarf in front of my mother. I felt so ashamed because it had been hers, one of the last gifts my father had given her. It would devastate her if I really lost it, and it was wrong not to ask for it back from you last night when I saw you'd picked it up."

"Why didn't you?"

"I—I'm not sure."

David shook his head slowly. "Don't try to lie, Harmony. I can tell you don't do it well."

"I'm a coward." She bowed her head. "I'm afraid to admit that I did it because I knew it would let me speak to you again."

"And you feel you need an excuse?"

She glanced at him from beneath her lashes. "You know I do, David." Sighing, she fingered the butterfly. "I stopped by Secondhand Treasures today. It was a delightful surprise. I had no idea Mrs. Silverman had anything so fine."

David watched her graceful fingers move over the gold. He thought of them moving so lightly over him and sucked in a deep breath. "She picked that up at an estate sale. Apparently she goes to a lot of them. Said the previous owner had been a woman whose husband grew a butterfly garden."

Looking as enchanted as she did confused, Harmony shook her head. "I'm not sure I know what that is."

"Neither did I. Apparently it's a garden made up of specific species of flowers that draw butterflies. He even had a stereo system built in to play the classical music they seemed to like best."

Her smile grew wider. "I remember my father talking about people who did things to coax ladybugs into their vegetable gardens to eat unwelcome insects, but I've never thought about an entire garden for butterflies!"

"It's a picturesque thought, isn't it?"

"Do you suppose he played them *Madame Butterfly?*" she asked whimsically.

To see her in this playful mood so soon after her frightening experience gave David such pleasure that he had to clench the hands in his pockets to keep from reaching out and touching the wind-reddened cheek he yearned to stroke and kiss. It wasn't fair, he thought. This was the season when gestures of warmth and affection were supposed to be as natural as eating too many cookies and drinking too much eggnog. Yet with Harmony even this small luxury was forbidden to him.

Realizing he still owed her an answer, he murmured, "Could be."

It was inevitable that she would pick up on his mood. Her sweet smile died and a slightly hunted look returned to her eyes. "I can't tell you what it means to me that you did this, David, but..." With a last longing look at the pin, she handed it back.

Hurt, he couldn't restrain his bitterness. "You mean you're afraid to." He ached for a world where they could talk without rebuke; where they could get to know one another without family interference; where they could touch without feeling as if they were doing something wrong. "I was hoping you would wear the pin so that whenever I saw you, I could remind myself that there's always tomorrow."

"Not for us."

"We're innocent, Harmony!"

"Shh—! David, *please*." She glanced around for anyone who might overhear, but for the moment they were the only people in the entryway. "Nothing can change the past." Her words were firm, but her voice was losing confidence fast. "Your uncle killed my father, and that kind of history lasts and...poisons, whether we want it to or not."

"But a thorough investigation determined that my uncle wasn't guilty of any misconduct."

Suddenly her whole bearing grew rigid, her eyes glittered. "*Misconduct?* How can you call murder anything less than what it is?"

"Because it wasn't murder, it was an *accident*, and deep in your heart you know that. Don't try to convince me that you don't," he insisted when it looked as if she wanted to protest. "It's bad enough that my uncle felt compelled to resign from the department, that he moved away from us and went all the way to Boston to find a job doing what he loves to do, work he's damned good at. Don't add to that injustice with your condemnation when you weren't even there that night!"

Indignant, she snapped, "Neither were you!"

"No, but at least—" Realizing what he'd been about to say, how self-righteous and arrogant he sounded, *who* he was lecturing, he closed his eyes and grimaced. "God, I'm sorry. This is exactly what I wanted to avoid, what I wanted to bring to an end between our families. We're above this, Harmony. We're not part of that ugliness."

"He was my *father*, David."

"I know. I know." And if it had been his father who had died, he wasn't sure he would be standing here. "All I can say is I believe that nothing grows in what's stagnant." He groped for another analogy. "It's the same with your music, isn't it? It can't be born in a vacuum, can it?" He stepped closer, so close he could smell the hyacinth fragrance in her hair, and his stomach clenched with deep-seated hunger. "Tell me you don't feel anything when we're close like this, and I'll try to walk away once and for all, try to forget you."

As he spoke he slowly eased the pin back into her hand and made her stiff, cold fingers close around it. Letting himself rub his thumb over her knuckles was a bonus. He drew something needed yet inexplicable from the act. He wasn't sure why, but this was familiar, as though they'd been like this, close, touching, many, many times before. What remained a mystery was whether it had occurred in a dream, a past life or a future one. He only knew this connection with her gave him confidence and strength. In her presence he felt whole.

"You can't do it, can you?" he said, relief and tenderness buoying him. "That's the way it is for me, too. It has been for a long time. I've tried not looking for you when I drive by the school, or at the supermarket if I'm running an errand for my mother, or at the bank or the post office. Even at church when we're both at the same service and I know I should be concentrating on the mass, I'm more interested in sneaking a glimpse of you up in the choir."

The rush of color in her cheeks and the lights twinkling behind her made her breathtaking. It was all he could do not to give in to his long-pent-up feelings and take advantage of the way her lips were parted in a soft O.

"Talk to me, Harmony. Tell me what you're feeling."

"Terror."

"There's nothing to be afraid of."

"David, have you told your family about me? About how you feel?"

He averted his gaze. Those gentle eyes saw too much. "No. But I think if they're told in the right way, they'd get used to the idea."

"You're not being honest, either," she replied, sadness adding a huskiness to her voice. "They'd be as shocked as mine would be. They'll never accept the idea."

"Let that be my problem." She needed to learn he could be as stubborn as her. More. "No one chooses who I see, and your family shouldn't dictate to you, either. So I'm going to ask you again . . . will you meet me? Will you go out with me?''

"Harmony?"

I can't. Please don't ask me again. I—

"Earth to zombie, woman . . . hey, in there! Anyone home?''

Harmony focused on the familiar face inching closer to peer at her. "Paula.''

"At last. It speaks,'' her friend intoned. She lifted her hand between them. "Now, how many fingers do you see?''

Jerking back her head before she went cross-eyed, Harmony grimaced and brushed the teasing blonde's hand away. "I get the message. I guess I was preoccupied and thought I was still the only one in here. Where did you come from?''

"Mars, from the way you were looking at me. Are you okay?''

"Yes, of course.'' But her heart was still racing from the residual emotions David had spawned last night. Hoping more didn't show, she retreated into the walk-in closet and took out the collar that went with her light blue choir robe. For all her lightheartedness, Paula Carlyle had a sharp eye, and Harmony wasn't prepared to explain herself. Not even to her closest friend. "I guess I'm not as caught up with my sleep as I thought I was. Between that extra rehearsal yesterday afternoon with the string quartet, so they can feel confident this afternoon when they play at the chamber of commerce's open house, and taking dear Mr. White's shift for the Salvation Army last night, I'm beat.''

Shaking her head, her vibrant, curvaceous friend slipped off her coat and reached for her own robe. "You should have stayed home and gotten a few more hours' sleep. As much as I'd miss your help on the high notes today, I'd prefer it to visiting you in the hospital."

"Just what I need, another mother," Harmony replied with a smile. She and Paula both taught at Appleton Junior-Senior High School, and on Sundays they sang soprano in the choir at All Saints. Sunny and sassy, Paula was popular with the senior girls who took her business classes, and they frequently used her as a sounding board and guidance counselor when they had something troubling them. Inevitably, Paula let that role carry over into her other relationships.

But Harmony loved her quick-witted friend, and since Paula's personal life, like her own, left something to be desired, they often spent weekends together, either shopping or going to the movies. Sometimes, when a three-day weekend allowed it, they took in a play down in Rutland or traveled up to Burlington.

"You'll have to excuse me for indulging my maternal instincts," Paula drawled, patting her short, permed hair after adjusting her own robe and collar. "One of my old college friends sent me a Christmas card with a picture of her new baby, and my biological clock has been whining ever since."

Glad to have something else to focus on besides herself, Harmony eyed her friend in the mirror as she lifted her longer hair from under the collar. "I wonder what Rod would say if I told him that."

"I've no idea, but you, dear heart, get an A for persistence." Paula's feline green eyes shadowed with a rare sadness. "It's useless, though. I had my chance with Rod the Intense, and I blew it."

"You didn't blow it, you just weren't ready."

"A mere technicality. The point is I've tried to let him know I made a mistake and he's playing deaf and blind." Paula turned away from the mirror, and her smile reemerged, brighter than ever. "Moving on to happier subjects, are you finished with your Christmas shopping?"

"I've barely started and already I have headaches. The twins have been begging for season ski lift tickets, but my mother's not thrilled. She's concerned that they're not giving their schoolwork enough attention, and I don't want to get in the middle of that argument."

"Smart girl. You know I think your mother's a wonder, but she can be such an ice queen when things don't go her way. You don't need that on top of everything else."

Harmony thought her mother had a good excuse for being strict and demanding but it wasn't a topic she wanted to get into just now. "Well, if I don't get them the passes, it'll only add two more headaches to my Christmas shopping list."

"Does that mean that if I ask you to drive up to Burlington with me next Saturday you'll go? We could leave early and make a day of it?"

More important, Harmony mused, it would get her away from Appleton. And David. "I'd like that," she said, as several other members of the choir entered the room.

"Good. It might help you forget being beaten up."

"I wasn't beaten up," she protested. But before she could finish correcting Paula, Denise Green, the organist, joined them.

"Tom and I just heard about what happened," she said, touching her cheek to Harmony's. "If we'd known last night when we saw you talking to David Shepherd, we would have stopped. Are you all right, dear? It was good of him to rise above his family's embarrassment and check on you."

Feeling an abrupt and surprising indignation on David's behalf, Harmony realized she couldn't say anything—not without sounding too passionate, too protective. Instead she replied, "He was returning the scarf I'd dropped the night before." Aware of Paula's speculative stare, she reached for her hymnal. "What, um, what are we singing today?"

The shift of topics worked, although even when they were seated in the mezzanine behind the altar, Harmony's thoughts remained on the scene that Denise had mentioned. Once again she and David hadn't parted well. But, she tried to insist to herself, it wasn't all her fault. Of all the places he'd chosen to confront her! Had anyone seen her clutching her scarf to her heart when she'd told him for the second—and she swore final—time that she couldn't, *wouldn't*, go out with him? Had they seen his face or hers when he'd stridden away from her?

Deep in thought, she didn't realize Paula was trying to get her attention until her friend literally reached behind her and tugged her to her feet by a handful of her robe. She groaned inwardly as she saw that everyone else in the choir was standing for their first song. Even though All Saints was a more relaxed, progressive Catholic church, her blunder wasn't unnoticeable, since she sat in the second row.

As she sprang to her feet she encountered the concerned gazes of her mother and grandmother, who, as always, were in one of the foremost pews. Her grandmother, looking very continental in her black lace mantilla, arched a graying eyebrow, and her mother frowned, the obvious question radiating in their eyes: *Are you all right?*

As she summoned a sheepish smile, Paula leaned close.

"What's the problem?" she whispered.

Denise had already begun the introductory bars to "Ave Maria," and to keep from missing the opening, Harmony simply shook her head to postpone the need to reply. But seconds after they began singing she felt her vocal cords fail her—precisely in the instant her gaze locked with David's.

He sat several rows behind her mother and grandmother. Since he was not famous for being a frequent attendee, she wasn't prepared to see him out there today. Not after last night. But there he sat with his family... staring holes into her. It was as if he was challenging her to deny his existence, and her emotions, all at the same time.

If anyone had asked her how or what she sang, she couldn't have answered. All she knew was that while her mouth moved and notes emerged, inside, her mind spun like a top gone out of control. She thought about the last question he'd asked her, his challenge that she be her own person, the responses he'd inspired when he'd touched her.

Once again she'd had to deny him, deny herself. Once again she'd let him down.

Harmony felt her hymnal shake in her hands and out of necessity passed it to Paula. To her relief her friend accepted it quickly, but shot her a sidelong look of concern. Her need to protect herself forced Harmony to ignore her, while inside she dealt with what David's presence might mean.

Here was a moment when a greater reservoir of knowledge about men would have come in handy. However, her experience with the opposite sex was limited. Music had always come first, then obtaining her teaching degree in order to be able to help support her family. That hadn't left much time for dating.

Not much had changed once she'd joined the work force, either, although this time because she'd realized she didn't want to date for the sake of going out. She'd simply felt no attraction to the men who had asked her—that is, until David. And, unlike the others, David Shepherd refused to be ignored.

Look at me, his gray eyes compelled as he gazed at her from his pew. *See me. See me for who I am.*

Why couldn't he see that what he wanted from her could never work out? Oh, yes, he would make her feel very feminine and alive. But that couldn't matter. Just as those youthful dreams of playing professionally couldn't be allowed to matter because of her familial responsibility.

If only her father had been less of a life-by-the-shirttails type of man and had thought to protect his family with a little more insurance. Then maybe there would have been enough money for tutors and the best schools her grandfather had hoped for her. But then, even *he* had not shown any great magnetic pull for money. He was heralded as one of the best violin teachers of his time, but bad investments and then costly hospitalization at the end of his life had devoured his modest estate.

Yes, her grandfather's and father's deaths had changed things considerably.

For how much longer? David's eyes challenged.

As their song ended and Father Bernard began greeting the congregation, Paula leaned closer and whispered, "You're whiter than your collar...and don't look now but a certain member of our police force in the sixth row doesn't look much better. What's going *on*, Harry?"

Even her friend's use of her brother's nickname for her didn't break her resolve. "Nothing."

"Right. And I'm Mother Teresa."

"Will you hush? You're attracting attention."

Paula made a guttural sound that let Harmony know who she thought was really the object of curiosity. But she was grateful that her friend remained unobtrusive for the rest of the service.

Once it was over, however, her mother and grandmother wasted no time in charging into the choir's dressing room. They each took an arm and escorted Harmony out.

"Maybe it's a delayed reaction," her mother said to her grandmother after ushering her down the aisle of the church.

"Whatever it is, we'll fix it. You come straight home and into bed," Gran Irena countered, barely braking in time to miss Father Bernard. "*Perdoni,* Father." She brushed him aside regally with her bag. "We've no time for small talk today. My granddaughter is not well."

Well used to matriarchs, the bespectacled priest managed to look properly regretful and saved his real concern for Harmony. "My dear, is there anything I can do? I had no idea you were suffering. You do look quite pale."

"*Grazie,* Father. But leave her to us," Gran Irena replied briskly. "We know how to care for our own."

They were as good as their word, and in truth Harmony didn't really mind the pampering, or the opportunity to sleep away the rest of the weekend. At least it let her escape herself.

By Monday she felt rested and ready to take on her regular schedule. It was a good thing, too; by the time she was heading out the school's doors late that afternoon she felt as if every drop of patience and energy had been wrung out of her.

"You look like I feel," Paula said, catching up with her on the way to the teachers' parking lot. "One of my graceful darlings managed to knock an electric typewriter off her desk this morning, and this afternoon the department computer decided to play hide-and-seek with my midyear exams for my fourth period class. If this was Friday I'd suggest we drive up to Burlington early, find a great restaurant and start the weekend off with a bottle of Chardonnay."

"Sounds as if you want to skip Christmas and head straight for New Year's." Harmony explained her own full day. "And to top that off my best piano accompanist informed me that her family's moving."

"Ouch. I know how much you valued her abilities." Paula shifted her loaded briefcase to her other hand, then patted Harmony's back. "At least you'll have her for the Christmas concert. Did you have time to make those calls about your grandfather's violin?''

"Yes, and I've made arrangements to send it off tomorrow. I've heard good things about this man," Harmony explained, grateful for her friend's interest. "But I know Gran Irena's going to go into shock. 'You're sending this *where?*' she'll start. Then there'll be this endless lecture filled with horror stories, the probability that we'll never see it again. And of course my mother will support her out of respect since the violin had been my grandfather's...."

"Tell them it's going to be your grandfather's unusable instrument if it's not properly cared for," Paula retorted before taking a deep breath of the crisp, late-afternoon air. "Oh, I need to mellow out. At least the snow is about gone." She gestured to her sporty coupé parked nearby. "Gosh, if I don't get my snow tires on before the next storm hits, I'm in trouble."

Harmony waged a silent battle with herself before suggesting, "Let me ask Rod if he'd do it for you?"

Paula looked anything but excited over the prospect. "Ah...you're sweet, but I don't think you'd better do that."

"Just because you two don't date anymore doesn't mean you can't be friends."

"In theory that sounds brilliant, but in practice... The truth is he makes me feel strange."

Startled, Harmony stopped in the middle of the parking lot and stared at her friend. Silhouetted by the late-afternoon sun, dressed in her business-conservative best, Paula looked sophisticated and capable from her gold swirl earrings to her smart navy leather pumps. "Strange? Rod? How?"

Paula groaned. "Harry—you're his sister!"

"Try to forget that for a minute. Strange how?"

"Something's still there, but it's embarrassing because I can feel his contempt, which I'm painfully aware is much stronger than his awareness of me as a woman."

It was a mouthful, even for Paula, but Harmony understood. And in its own way, it paralleled some of her feelings for David. "Why haven't you said that before?"

"I *have*. But you once told me that the only way you could be his sister and my best friend was if we didn't drag you into our mess."

"That was almost five years ago, Paula! We were barely dry behind our ears back then."

"Well, some of us more than others," her friend drawled, tongue in cheek. Then she grew serious. "Never mind. I know what I'm doing. Rod's a lot like you. Serious. No-nonsense. He was ready to settle down before I even *entered* college. You're right about me. I'd just wanted some time out. Fun."

"He understands, Paula. He may not come out and say that—"

"I know, I know." Waving her hand to dismiss what she'd said, Paula thought for a moment. "I guess we would have broken up regardless, but I didn't have to hurt him as badly as I did."

Impressed with her friend's compassion and understanding, Harmony laid her hand over Paula's. "Maybe you need to tell him that someday. Maybe if he agrees to do your tires for you that would give you the chance."

"Maybe the moon is really a coconut cream pie. God, Harry, you have to be the world's biggest dreamer. I don't think—"

Harmony saw Paula's eyes widen at the same moment she heard the vehicle pulling in to the lot. It gave her a strange feeling creeping up the back of her neck.

"Uh-oh," Paula murmured. "Speaking of intense men . . . isn't that the white knight himself?"

She didn't want to turn and look. All she could do was close her eyes and pray, *Please don't let it be him. Please* . . .

Chapter Four

"Nice try, but I don't think ignoring him is going to work," Paula muttered to Harmony. "I doubt he's going to go away."

Harmony didn't think her heart could sink much lower, but it plummeted another level. "Whatever happens, don't leave me. Promise?"

"You can't be serious."

She understood her friend's incredulous stare. Even with her family's history with the Shepherds, this had to be a great deal to ask. "I can't explain right now, just believe me when I say I don't want to be alone with him."

That clearly wasn't good enough for Paula. "Why not? Is there something sleazy about this guy that you haven't told me about?"

The thought that anyone could think David was less than honorable and committed made Harmony leap to his defense. "Of course not! He's wonderful!"

"He is?"

Couldn't she understand anything? "That's the problem, Paula. He's *too* wonderful."

"Oh. Oh! Good grief, Harry. What have I been doing, hibernating? I didn't realize you had it *that* bad. Your family is going to bust a gut if they get wind of this."

"That's what I've been trying to tell you." She cast her friend an entreating look. "Does that mean you'll help me?"

As David pulled up beside them, Paula muttered out of the side of her mouth, "Are you kidding? I wouldn't miss this for the world."

Harmony didn't have time to reply because David was getting out of his car. As usual he wasn't wearing a hat, and his blond hair burned like silver-streaked gold in the late-afternoon sun; however, nothing caught her attention as fast as his broad, leather-encased shoulders as he straightened and stood squarely before them.

"Ladies."

Although he spoke to both of them, he had eyes only for Harmony. Meeting his gaze took more courage than she thought she possessed. Surely he wasn't going to make a scene here? She didn't mind that Paula knew, but what about anyone else still inside the school?

"Is something wrong, Officer Shepherd?"

"Officer Shepherd?" Paula uttered in disbelief. "Harry, please. Let's not carry this too far."

She didn't know what to say. This was what Paula considered standing by her?

"It's all right...Paula, isn't it?" David tore his eyes away from Harmony long enough to offer a winning smile.

Paula's expression could only be described as bliss-ful. "I had no idea you knew me."

Disgruntled that her closest friend was doing ev-erything but preening, Harmony replied flatly, "Da-vid's thoroughness is second to nothing—particularly his timing."

He shook his head at her although the tenderness in his eyes remained. "I haven't even told you why I'm here, and already you're out to punish me."

She didn't want to feel ashamed, but he managed to undo her temper and confidence all at the same time. Oh, Lord, she suddenly thought, had she jumped to the wrong conclusion? Had something happened? "What's wrong?"

"Nothing that deserves that look on your face. It's merely a technicality. But I need you to come with me to the station."

The thought of having to return there gave her chills. "Why?"

"There's a minor problem with some statement you made when you were at headquarters the other eve-ning. It shouldn't take more than a few minutes."

That explanation sounded reasonable enough, if frustrating. Except when she considered who was de-livering the message. "It's unusual for you to be working this shift, isn't it? I thought you worked later?"

"Normally. But the flu's starting to affect our manpower. I offered to take a double shift for a day or two to let some of the married guys with families off the hook."

Another wave of shame swept over her. Here she was being concerned about his motivations, only to learn they were of the highest caliber. "That's...very generous of you."

"Very," Paula echoed, stepping away from them. "Um, Harmony, I just remembered an errand I have to run, so I'll leave you to it. Maybe I'll give you a call later and we can firm up our date, okay?"

Panic struck Harmony anew. After what she'd told her, how could Paula leave? "Do you really have to run?"

"Absolutely. I also have a steno quiz to grade and a library book to finish that's due back tomorrow...."

"Not to mention giving your cat a bath," Harmony noted, although Paula didn't own a cat and was in fact allergic to them. But she wanted her friend to know how she felt about this sudden desertion.

"Oh... *Kitty*...don't remind me." With an uneasy smile and wave, Paula all but ran for her car.

Deserted, that's how she felt. But Harmony reached deep inside for the strength she needed to endure. She could handle this. It wasn't as though she would actually have to deal with him alone.

"If you'd like to get in, I'll drive you over."

Had he been reading her mind and decided to toy with her? "Why? I mean, can't I take my own car?"

He scratched his right eyebrow, his expression thoughtful. "I suppose you could, except that they asked me specifically to get you there. But... I guess you could follow me if that's what you need to do."

She *needed* to get away from him as soon as possible, before she forgot all the real and valid reasons. She certainly knew how to find the police station as well as he did. However, grateful to be able to put some distance between them, Harmony summoned a smile. "Thank you, I will. And David...?" She moistened her unusually dry lips. "I'm sorry about the other evening. I don't mean to be hard. Or cruel."

The soft look he gave her nearly stopped her heart. "You couldn't be either if you tried."

She didn't know how she made it to her car. Her legs felt like mush the whole way. Somehow, though, she managed, and again wishing that things could be different for them, she started the engine and obediently backed from her parking slot and followed him out onto the street.

It proved oddly satisfying to drive behind him. What an excuse it gave her to study him, to allow her curiosity free rein. It let her fantasize, and dream. Safe, she could admit that if things were different they might have been allowed to explore these feelings between them. Preoccupied, she didn't realize they were going in the wrong direction, that the woods were growing more dense, until the trees ultimately surrounded them.

What was he doing? She began to worry profusely as they passed the city limits. The only reason she could think for him to be taking her this way was if there was some kind of road closing in town that necessitated an auxiliary route.

Impossible, she told herself with the next calming breath she took. She kept up with town business and she hadn't read about any roadwork planned between now and Christmas—barring emergencies, that is.

Something told her that there hadn't been any emergencies.

When she spotted the rest stop up ahead, she signaled him with her lights. To her relief, he turned. Then she noticed how isolated and shadowy an area it was, and she wished he'd kept going. Even as he climbed out and looked around, she knew there was time to escape. But she was too angry. Intent on giving him a piece of her mind, she sprang from her car.

"Just what do you think you're doing?"

"Making sure I get to talk to you."

Talk? "You lied to me, David!" As much as she despised the weakness, she couldn't keep her voice from trembling. "You've treated me like a fool."

"I would never do that!"

"What's this?" she demanded, arms spread. When he failed to answer, she wheeled around and walked. She was determined to get back to her car, to get out of there and never, never, *never* believe anything anyone ever told her again.

"Harmony." David caught her by her upper arm and swung her around. "Harmony, wait!"

"Let me go!"

"Not yet. Hear me out first."

"How dare you even ask that!"

"All right, I understand you being upset, but tell me what else I was supposed to do. Would you have come with me if I'd asked you politely?"

"Of course not."

"Then I did the right thing."

"What you did could get you fired! Do you realize I could file charges against you?"

"Yes. If that's what you want to do."

It was hardly what she'd been expecting, and just one more contradiction to the judgments she and her family had placed against the name Shepherd. "You're crazy."

He drew a long breath. "Could be. But if I am, you're driving me there." He shifted his hold, slipping one arm around her waist.

Maybe if he'd been angry, or if she'd seen anything violent in his eyes, she might have resisted, fought him. But he was gentle, oh, so gentle, and that's what made her hesitate and doubt herself.

"Tell me one last time that you intend to let what's between us dry up like all these dead leaves," he demanded gruffly. "Tell me that's what you want."

"This has nothing to do with want. Why can't you accept that?"

"Because I've tried to look at things your way and I can't. Because if you ask me to walk away from you, to leave you alone forever, you might as well ask me to stop breathing."

Perhaps she would have thought of something else to say. But giving her no time to even recover, to think, he kissed her.

He would stop breathing? Even as Harmony fought for breath she knew he was wrong, wrong! She'd stopped the moment she'd realized his intentions. Nothing, however, prepared her for the feel of his body against hers, the impact of his lips seeking and claiming, the rush of heat and the wave of emotions that lifted and engulfed her.

It shouldn't have happened. She shouldn't have let it. But then there was only David...David. Like the man himself, his name swept through her, as yearning as his kiss, as strong as the arms that nearly lifted her off the ground, as indomitable as the body that made it clear what he wanted and that there was nowhere to run.

But why on earth would she want to escape? How could she, when suddenly all that seemed to matter was right here? She wanted this moment to go on and on . . . she wanted these feelings to last forever.

She forgot that she was supposed to be upset with him. Instead there was relief that they were away from town on a road that was rarely used except on weekends when ski buffs raced for the beauty and speed of the Green Mountains' slopes.

"Oh, God, I've wanted this for so long. You don't know how long," David rasped, sliding a kiss across her cheek, then burying his face against her hair. "I can't believe it's finally happening."

She was beginning to believe. And it was good . . . so good.

He sought her lips again. She'd never dreamed it could be like this . . . to be wanted this much . . . enough to let her resistance be chipped away layer by layer, leaving her feeling naked, reduced to a creature of wanting. She'd never imagined it was possible to be this vulnerable. She'd believed only her music could tap her innermost feelings. But as he parted her lips and slipped his tongue deep like a man dying of thirst, she soon learned she was wrong. Truly, no one had ever kissed her with such need and hunger. He redefined the word *desire* for her. At the same time he maintained a control over himself that was the epitome of concern and respect. Had any woman ever felt more cherished?

She must have made some sound because David lifted his head again, just enough to look deep into her eyes. Shifting to caress her lips and cheeks with his thumbs, he whispered, "Harmony . . . beautiful Harmony."

"You'd better stop. You're making me dizzy."

"Good."

"But I can't think."

"That's even better. Anything else?"

She would have laughed if she'd had the strength. He really was sweet. But all she could do was gaze up at him and wonder, *How can this be?*

David understood Harmony's bedazzled expression. Relief and joy were making him feel not quite earthbound, too. Already resigned to the idea that he would never manage to win her confidence on a legitimate level, he'd decided to try to steal her heart through fantasy. To suddenly discover it was working, to be rewarded with the answer to his dreams in the flesh was almost more than a mortal man could take in.

He was, however, a fast learner.

Drawing her to him again, he lowered his head. His heart filled when this time she didn't use her clenched hands as a barrier between them, but slipped her arms around his neck and urged him closer. She made him wish she hadn't been wearing gloves so he could feel her explore, experiment and discover the texture of his hair, realize that his heart was pounding as violently as it had the night he'd seen her attacked by those two thugs. But as his shoulder muscles tightened spasmodically at her touch, he knew he wouldn't complain. Any gesture on her part was generous, wonderful. More than enough. In fact, he still needed to get used to how deeply she affected him. Just these few moments were making him feel drugged.

His good intentions, however, were forgotten as she shyly touched her tongue to his lips. With a groan he yielded to her invitation and reduced himself to a creature of sensation.

Harmony... Harmony... Her name was a song in his heart. His body trembled with it. That might have embarrassed him if she'd been anyone else, if she'd been someone more experienced, shrewd, jaded. But this lovely woman was sweet and generous. He wouldn't have been falling this hard for her if she was anything less.

All his life he'd wanted someone to call his own. He'd been searching for her. Careful to protect his secret, he'd stumbled through the first several years of adulthood not even certain from where such intent, let alone need, had come. He'd had a happy family life while growing up, despite the tragedy that had cut his uncle from the nucleus of their existences. His parents had been strict but caring. His four sisters still filled the range from endearing to crazy-fun just as they had all the years he'd been plastering bandages on their knees while teaching them the rudiments of touch football, then how to drive and finally enough of the mysteries about men so as not to scare off their boyfriends. But something had always been missing. Now he understood what—or rather *who*.

He'd been waiting for Harmony. It was that simple, and that complex. It made him want to throw his head back and laugh in triumph, and at the same time sweep her into his arms and run for someplace safe because knowing what you wanted didn't mean you had a right to have it, that you automatically had a right to a happily-ever-after ending.

Once again he eased back to look at her. Studying her lovely face, examining her dark eyes, he wondered if she was ready for all that was in his heart.

"No. Oh, God, I don't think I could take any more right now."

Had she taken up mind reading or was he frightening her by exposing, asking for too much too soon? "I'm not sure I understand, and I *know* I don't like the fear I see in your eyes. What's wrong, Harmony? I could feel that you enjoyed me kissing you. You kissed me back."

"I know, I know." She sighed and rubbed her forehead. "But can't we let that be enough for a while? This *is* wonderful, and I'll remember it no matter what happens in the future."

"Hell, that sounds like goodbye!" With panic tasting like metal in his mouth, he tightened his hold—as if that would be enough. How did you hold a dream? "Do you realize what I risked to get a few minutes alone with you? Do you think I can go back, pretend I don't know you? Let you try to ignore me?"

"That's not what I'm asking. I…I don't know what I want," she groaned, shaking her head. "All I know is that I'm afraid, and I can't be rushed into anything."

"Harmony, you've been running away from me for most of these twelve years. How can you suggest asking to spend time with you makes me guilty of rushing you?"

He could almost hear her repeating his words in her mind. Then she shook her head, as if it were too much to comprehend. Or that she couldn't let it matter.

"I just don't want to be pressured," she entreated, her gaze imploring. "I don't want to make any promises when neither of us are sure we can keep them! Can't we simply accept the moment and leave it there?"

"And then what? What happens the next time our paths cross in town and you happen to be with your mother or someone else in your family? Are you going to turn away and pretend I don't exist, the way they will?"

"David, that's awful!"

His portable radio crackled, keeping him from assuring her that he agreed wholeheartedly. Muttering a curse, he went to use the one in his car, certain he was too far out of town for a decent reception. As expected, the dispatcher was concerned that he hadn't checked in yet. It was minutes past his allotted break time. He made some lame excuse and assured her that he was back on duty, silencing his conscience by reminding himself how much time he donated to the department. Time that never appeared on his time sheets.

Frustrated because he could take only one more minute with Harmony, he returned to where she stood standing with her clasped hands pressed to her lips. Her lovely, oval face glowed from the radiance of the sinking sun, but she looked forlorn, and as pensive as he felt.

He sighed. "I have to go."

"I assumed you did."

"I won't lie and say I'm not disappointed. I wanted more from this. I want more from *you*." Hoping not to frighten her, he carefully took hold of her shoulders. "But we'll do it your way. Hell, I'll do whatever you want if it means giving us a chance. You *do* want to do that, don't you?" he asked, ducking his head trying to see her eyes under the dense veil of her lashes.

"I shouldn't admit this, and I'm so afraid I'm going to regret it, but..."

"You won't," he said urgently as he drew her close one last time.

"It won't be wise, David."

He managed a crooked smile because although she sounded doubtful, she didn't resist being near him. "We've tried wise, angel eyes," he said, shifting to dig into his jacket. Withdrawing his hand, he offered her the butterfly pin he'd tried to give her a few days ago. "And don't say no to this, either."

Carefully pinning it to the scarf near her throat, he murmured, "I want something of mine near you. When I see you touch it, I'm going to imagine you're touching me." That earned him her most relaxed smile yet.

"I had no idea you were such a romantic man, David Shepherd."

"I didn't think I was. Being around you inspires me. There." He leaned back to inspect his handiwork. "Made for you," he murmured, his gaze admiring.

Her eyes grew soft, dreamy as she fingered the pin. "Thank you. It really is beautiful and I'll treasure it."

A lump growing in his throat, he embraced her one last time and pressed a kiss to her hair. "I have to let you go and get back to work."

"Yes. Don't get into trouble over me, David. I couldn't bear being responsible for that."

"I told you, where you're concerned, I've been in trouble for ages. Ah, God... Just one more kiss," he whispered, lowering his head. "One more and maybe I can get through the rest of the day."

Seeming as eager as he was to experience the magic again, she rose on tiptoe. Her arms slid willingly around his neck and she gave him the slight weight of her body with an innocent's trust. David had a feeling she was innocent, and his heart filled with emotion even as the warmth of her lips seeped into him.

When his ever-present hunger coaxed him into deepening the kiss, the ache in the pit of his stomach spread wider and lower. To assuage it, he drew her closer, between his legs and into the cradle of his hips. Then he plumbed the sweet, silky depths of her mouth. He wanted to seep the memory of her into his mind and engrave himself in her heart. As expected, it soon reduced him to a purely physical being, his shallow breaths the only sound except for the pounding of his heart in his ears.

He didn't hear the car until it was too late. The screech of brakes had the same chilling effect on him as the cocking of a handgun, and David instinctively drew Harmony behind him, not knowing what to expect.

"Damnation!" he muttered, staring at the sedan that had stopped on the two-lane highway.

"Mrs. Silverman," Harmony groaned, peering around him.

Actually, it was difficult to determine who was behind the steering wheel. It was only the ancient butter-yellow Cadillac that gave them the strong hint. Obviously she'd been to an estate sale or something; the vehicle was virtually weighted down to the rims with an incredible amount of new finds for her shop.

"I wish she'd move before the windows shatter and an axle snaps," David noted, feeling anything but generous at the moment.

As if she'd heard him, the old woman gunned the engine and took off. All she left behind was a dark cloud of burned oil.

Harmony stepped out from around David and touched a hand to her throat. "David, what are we going to do?"

Chapter Five

"*Try not to worry. I'll think of something.*"

"*David, she's a sweet lady, but the biggest gossip in town. This will get back to our families. We won't have any control over how they find out. It'll be awful!*"

"*I'll talk to her. Try not to worry, sweetheart.*"

"*David, you're beginning to worry me.*"

Momentarily abandoning his thoughts of Harmony and their last conversation, he summoned an innocently perplexed smile for his mother as she placed a glass of milk before him. "Why's that, Mom?"

"You don't hear half of what anyone says to you these days. I might as well be talking to that refrigerator there." She tilted her blond head toward the aging model directly across from the dinette table. "At least it makes groans and grunts like your father when he watches his ball games and pretends to be interested in what I'm saying."

As his mother took her seat at the oblong table opposite his father, David caught his youngest sister, Shawna, ducking her head to hide a smirk. Was that simple pleasure, her response to seeing him get nagged for a change instead of her, or did she know something? Only too aware of how sneaky she could be, he knew he had more to worry about from her.

"Leave the boy alone, Barbra," his father said, helping himself to a center slice of the meat loaf on the platter before him. "Just because he's thirty years old, single and prefers living at home doesn't mean we have the right to grill him. He's working double shifts these days. For crying out loud, if he was anything less than preoccupied, *I'd* be worried about him. Stop being a mother or he may decide it's not such a waste to live on his own."

Knowing full well what was coming, David swallowed his response along with a mouthful of mashed potatoes before accepting the meat platter from his parent. If he was lucky, he mused as his father shot him a conspiratorial wink, he could sit back and enjoy his dinner while his mother and dad entertained them all with their easygoing ribbing.

"Listen to you. I *am* a mother, Glenn, and as such I reserve the right to be concerned about my children no matter how old they are."

"She means nag and fuss," his father offered helpfully.

With his mouth twitching to hold back a grin and his dark blond hair tumbling over a barely lined forehead, his father looked far younger than his fifty-eight years, David thought. Three years younger, trim and energetic, his mother was also aging with grace. How they were managing it with all the headaches and heartbreak they'd suffered through the years, he didn't know, but he was grateful to have inherited those genes. He could just imagine the beautiful children he and Harmony could make.

"*Nag?* I do not nag, Glenn Shepherd. Shawna," his mother moaned without taking a breath, "what do I have to do, beg? One spoonful of potatoes and a small slice of meat loaf will not be the end of the world. I don't care if you do have the female lead in the *Nutcracker*, you can't live on salad and yogurt."

Nineteen-year-old Shawna lifted her chin and elegantly slid another bite of lettuce seasoned in lemon juice and pepper into her mouth. The act accentuated the curve in her swanlike neck and best exposed the gamin profile that had won her the role, which typically went to a younger girl. "It's only for another few weeks, Mother. Calm down. You don't want your youngest child to be the first ballerina in the history of the production to have cellulite, do you?"

"You mean I get a vote?"

Like David, these two Shepherd women had inherited most of the silver highlights in their hair, while his other three sisters were darker toned like his father. As his mother leaned closer to Shawna, and blue eyes challenged blue-gray, he compared pert-nosed profiles and silently thought, *Yup. Good genes*.

Shawna's sharper chin trembled with laughter, and with a melodramatic sniff she turned back to her salad. "Nope. Just doing my sisterly good deed of the day and making conversation to help my big brother escape any more interrogating."

Had he thought her an imp? The rascal was a shark. With his heart thudding and questions burning in his mind, David struggled to keep an indifferent look on his face as he met her sly grin. "Excuse me? What's that supposed to mean?"

"That's what I'd like to know," their father echoed with a confused frown.

"Merely that while I may be the youngest member of this family, that doesn't mean that I'm the least observant. I don't think big Dave's preoccupation is a result of job pressure at all." Her blue-gray eyes twinkled with wicked glee as she glanced around the table. "Hasn't anyone else figured that out?"

"What could possibly be more important than focusing on your job?" their father asked, a fork full of green beans hovering inches in front of his mouth. As a former cop himself, and now head of security at the nearby junior college, he took great pride in having always given one hundred percent to an employer.

"Oh, Glenn, really," David's mother chided. "Shawna's talking about girls. About *relationships*."

David steeled himself for his mother's anxious inspection. "Is it true, dear? We thought you were happy living here with us?"

While David was amused to think that she'd hadn't shed a tear when three of his sisters had married and left home, it was his father who burst into hearty laughter.

"You're one for the books, Barb. Of course he's happy here, but there comes a time when a man has to move on. Start thinking about getting a family of his own. Why, Toni's been married nearly ten years, Lea for, what—? Four? And our tomboy Jolene, who we thought we would have to pay to marry off, has even been out of the house for nearly a year."

Although she still looked worried, David's mother held up a finger. "That reminds me, we need to get the rooms over the garage straightened up. Jolene phoned today and said she and Jack will be coming in from New York two weeks before Christmas."

"There goes my weekend," David's father groaned. "How's a guy supposed to miss his kids when they're underfoot all the time?"

Relieved that the conversation had moved away from him, David quickly interjected, "If you need my room, Mom, let me know. With my schedule I won't mind bunking on the couch for the duration."

"Smooth move, bro," Shawna teased. "We won't tell her that would make it all the easier for you to sneak in and out."

"Quiet, you shrimp-size bag of bones."

"I hit a nerve . . . I hit a nerve!"

As she sang, their mother's expression turned into one of complete exasperation. "Shawna, really. It's beyond me how anyone with so much discipline for dance can be totally uncontrollable when under this roof."

"It must be a fungus in the heating unit affecting her brain," David suggested, with a tolerance born of love and pride for his talented sibling. "Speaking of Christmas, has anyone heard from Uncle Douglas? Do you think he'll be coming out this year?"

He asked the question every Christmas and each time his father replied, "It's not likely, son. You know when Douglas quit the department here, he swore he would never be back."

"But that was then," his mother offered with more optimism as she paused in breaking a dinner roll in half. "This fourth wife seems to be giving him a sense of stability and strength. I wouldn't write him off yet, dear."

"And if she doesn't work out, there's always time to try number five," Shawna said impishly.

That earned her a disapproving glance from both parents. "That's not amusing in the least," her mother added. "Your uncle has had a terrible time dealing with what happened, and bad luck on top of that. It was enough that those Martins made sure he was a mental wreck when he left Appleton. First a divorce, then his second wife dies in that dreadful car wreck, followed by another divorce.... I know it's Christmas, and we're supposed to have a feeling of goodwill toward men and all, but when I think of how unreasonably cruel Olivia Martin was, not to mention that nasty son of hers—"

"Mom." David paused to temper his words, aware of how suspicious his family would become if he protested too vehemently. "That's ancient history. We can't expect the Martins to change if we aren't willing to."

"Personally I don't care what they do. We did our best to be sympathetic and tolerant, but even after they made sure your poor father was permanently separated from his only brother, they've treated each and every one of us as if we have blood on our hands."

David couldn't say anything. If he tried, he knew his true feelings for Harmony would come out, and this was definitely not the right moment. He stared at the food on his plate that he now didn't know if he could finish.

His father cleared his throat, and said, "Let's talk of happier things, dear. Don't upset yourself. Everything will work out one of these days."

He brought up a yearly topic, namely what size Christmas tree to purchase. David stopped listening.

He knew the routine. His mother would suggest, then debate all the reasons they should have a small, table-top one for a change, and his father would argue, but in the end they would find the biggest in the county because their roomy, two-story house would seem barren with anything less. In the same way, the holidays wouldn't feel complete if the entire family wasn't together. That just reminded him of all that was on the line because of these impossible feelings he bore for Harmony Martin.

"Are you ready to pluck my head bald and dip me in Limburger cheese?"

"No. But I may glue your leotards to your toe shoes."

Draping herself photogenically against the door-jamb, Shawna watched him as he put on his holster and gun. He was scheduled for the night shift tonight and had to be downtown in fifteen minutes.

"I was only trying to snap you out of your slump, David."

"I didn't know I was in one."

"Okay, so I was fishing."

Now, he thought, maybe he would find out exactly what she knew instead of worrying himself into an ulcer. "No kidding?"

She nibbled on her lower lip. "Teasing aside, I do approve. Of you getting serious, that is."

Oh, no, she hadn't a clue. His answering smile was wry. "Only because you want me gone so you can have my room."

"That, too. But seeing you happy is more important. Is there any hope?"

An increasingly familiar ache gripped his chest. Ah, Lord, he prayed silently, he hoped so. But aloud he responded, "Stay tuned." Cuffing her lightly under her chin, he slipped past her and headed down the hall.

"Wait a minute!" The shifting air made more sound than her footsteps did as she raced after him. "You're not going to tell me who she is?" she cried, incredulous.

"Who who is?"

"C'mon, David. I swear I won't tell."

"Tell what?"

"I won't. Promise!"

"That's rich. If there is someone—and I'm not saying there is—you'd be the last person I'd tell. You haven't kept a secret since you were seven."

"Seven? Ha!"

"It was the year we all chipped in to get Mom that birthstone ring. I worked the paper route for John Templeton, the girls did various baby-sitting jobs, and *you* hit Mom up for a raise in your allowance. Forget it, kiddo."

Shawna leaned back against the wall at the top of the stairs and pursed her lips for a silent whistle. "Whoever she is, this sounds serious."

Heaven save him from little sisters. "I hope your thighs grow to be the size of mine... and twice as hairy."

"Fink. And don't think you're going to keep your secret for long. The CIA would kill to have my contacts," she called after him.

"Sweet dreams, Twinkletoes. See you tomorrow."

* * *

"Hello, stranger. I haven't seen you in a few days. Are you hiding from me?"

Framed by her gangly brothers, Harmony froze for a moment and stared at Mrs. Silverman, who blocked their way. Always a colorful dresser, tonight she wore a green satin baseball jacket over polyester stirrup pants, a raspberry boa and a natty violet felt fedora. The woman looked as if she'd stepped right out of a scene from *Auntie Mame,* and Harmony could sense her brothers' incredulous reactions. "Why, no, Mrs. Silverman. What a strange thing to say. I've just been busy. Guys, this is Mrs. Silverman, who owns Secondhand Treasures, the lady I told you about who was so kind to me the night I was mugged. This is Christopher and Brandon," she added, introducing the old lady to the twins.

They mumbled the obligatory greetings their mother had long been drilling into them and earned an approving beam from the elderly woman. "What handsome young men. No one can look at you Martins and not tell you're family," Gladys said, pinching each agonized boy on the cheek. Then she focused on Harmony. "You aren't playing tonight? I've missed hearing your little street concerts."

"I'm not scheduled again until the weekend of Christmas. It's because I have the concerts at school to prepare for."

"I see, yes. That's wonderful, dear. And it looks as if you've recovered from your traumatic experience. I don't think I've ever seen you look lovelier."

"Thank you. You're very kind to say that."

"In fact, if I didn't know any better, I would think you were falling in love." She grabbed each of the boys' sleeves. "Let me tell you, youngsters, and listen to me because you can't begin learning about such things soon enough. There's nothing like a beau to bring out the blossoms in a girl's cheeks. If you ever have any doubts about your own sweethearts, let that be a signal to you."

Harmony didn't know what to say. What was the woman doing?

Aware of her brothers' curious looks, she could barely manage to breathe, let alone think of something that would put an end to this. Why was Mrs. Silverman baiting her? What had she done to deserve this? She'd always tried to be kind to her when their paths crossed; she even *liked* her for sticking to her own style, although most people thought the woman slightly off the wall.

This conversation had to be stopped before the twins started picking up anything. "Really, Mrs. Silverman. I'm flattered that you—"

"Don't worry, darling. I'm only indulging in a little harmless chitchat."

Harmless? She had two of the sharpest teenagers on earth for brothers. It had been ages since she'd bluffed them during a game of poker, let alone something serious. How was she supposed to convince them that Mrs. Silverman was simply rambling?

"Maybe you boys aren't aware of this, but I'm a widow with no children of my own. You can't imagine what joy it is for me to get to visit with you two and your lovely sister."

What on earth was the woman working up to? Harmony sensed something in the wind, but she couldn't put her finger on it.

"In fact," Mrs. Silverman continued, touching a finger to her rouged, wrinkled cheek, "you've given me an idea. I've decided to do a bit of entertaining for the holidays. Even in a friendly town like Appleton we have our share of lonely souls around the holidays, don't we?"

Although Harmony managed a smile and a nod, she winced inwardly, hoping Gladys wasn't going to ask her to attend this event or, worse yet, to entertain the guests with a concerto or two.

"But let's face it, sweetheart, I'm not a very good planner."

"Well, Mrs. Silverman, it's often sincerity and goodwill that make a party a success," Harmony replied, feeling somewhat queasy.

Nodding, the woman continued, "Exactly. Sincere. That's why I want you to come over one evening and help me plan something. You're such a sophisticated young woman—"

"You are?" Christopher asked with astonishment, ever the wise guy.

"I know you'd be able to solve all of my problems in no time at all."

Giving her young brother an elbow in the ribs for his brashness, she struggled for the appropriate response. *Tell her yes and run. You can always think of an excuse later.*

Except she never behaved that way.

She opened her mouth to try anyway, but realized her first hunch was right. She couldn't do it.

"Mrs. Silverman . . . the problem is that I'm helping the boys with their Christmas shopping tonight, and tomorrow—"

"Oh, I had no intention of intruding on such short notice, darling."

She almost sighed in relief. "I appreciate that."

"How's Friday for you? It's a very good day for me. In fact, I think by then I could get someone to go over to that roadside park north of town—you know the one I mean?—and cut a clump of mistletoe for me to use in decorating. I was by there the other day and, sweetheart, you would not believe the abundance of mistletoe growing out there."

This was turning into a nightmare, all right. What was ironic was that on Friday she'd planned to go to Burlington with Paula. But her friend had already called with the news that her car had broken down and needed to go in for repair. Between that expense and her Christmas list, Paula told her, she was going to have to settle for shopping in town. That left Harmony with no excuse to turn down Gladys's request—though it felt more like blackmail.

"Would you believe that's a perfect day for me, too?" she murmured, unable to add the smile the line required.

"Great," Brandon added, clapping his hands together. "It's perfect for everyone!"

"Then I'll see you at seven," Mrs. Silverman said with a soft laugh. "Oh—and don't eat."

"No?"

"Nothing. We'll be in the middle of Hanukkah and I thought I might try a few of my favorite recipes on you. If you think they're too exotic, we can experiment from there."

"Well. I'm sure we'll come up with something."

"Indeed. And I've kept you long enough. Good night, dear. Boys, it was a pleasure."

As Harmony stood there wondering how she would warn David about all this, Brandon asked, "What do you think she means by exotic, sis?"

"It sounds kinda fishy to me," Christopher muttered. "If I were you, Harmony, I'd make sure I ate a big lunch just in case."

Tugging her ebony-haired siblings with her, she hurried away. The sooner she put some distance between them, she assured herself, the sooner she could get the boys' minds on something else. Christopher, however, was in no hurry to change the subject.

"What was she talking about when she mentioned being in love, sis? I thought you'd sworn off men after Gran tried to fix you up with old Mr. Columbo's son?"

"I said that because Stan Columbo was in worse shape than his father," she replied, unable to resist shivering at the memory of the tobacco-chewing plumber who serviced their house. "As for what Mrs. Silverman said, you can't take it all to heart. She's getting on in years and sometimes gets carried away."

"She seems pretty together to me, even if she does dress funny," Brandon offered.

That's what she was worried about, Harmony thought as she increased her pace down the street toward the decorated shops. But she would have to wait until Friday to learn what was up.

"Things can get confusing after sundown. Since you're a newcomer to Appleton, I'll let you off with a warning this time, sir, but in the future please remember that making a U-turn downtown is illegal. Good night."

With a polite nod to the relieved man and woman in the van, David stepped away from the vehicle and watched it ease down the road. A nice couple. Newlyweds, he thought wistfully, remembering how much they'd touched and patted each other as they waited for him to run a license check. They deserved a break, he decided, hoping that down the line someone would reciprocate.

As he continued down the street he couldn't help wonder what Harmony was doing tonight. The ringing bell from the Salvation Army volunteer farther up the block only made him miss her more. It was terrible not to be able to pick up a telephone and chat for a few minutes. Three days...it had been three days since he'd last seen her, touched her, drawn her scent and her tastes deep. It felt more like a dream now than an actual experience. If he didn't see her again soon, he was going to go out of his mind.

He'd been fighting calling her. Yesterday he'd lost the battle, picked up the phone at the station and dialed her number. A woman had answered—her grandmother, he believed. He'd hung up without saying anything. He hated people who did that, but he hadn't wanted to cause trouble for Harmony.

They needed to talk, about that and other things. They had to come to some kind of an agreement. He refused to give up.

Turning down Maple Street he saw a bent form up ahead. The roads were fairly well lit there, but without the traffic that was on Main Street. He narrowed his eyes and realized it was a woman...elderly...and struggling with a two-wheeled wagon. He hurried his pace and identified it as one of those old shopping-cart contraptions his grandmother had used. Then he noted the woman's attire.

Lord. That was Gladys Silverman up ahead.

He spun around and thought about running back to Main Street, but he couldn't budge.

What are you doing, Shepherd?

It was his job to patrol the streets of Appleton. *All* the streets. Maybe he wasn't looking forward to an encounter with the old woman right now. Maybe he was even afraid of her. But he had no right to forget that she was a citizen of this community, and elderly. That wagon was loaded down and too much for her to handle. The least he could do was help her get it into her building.

He turned again and retraced his steps, this time hurrying to reach her. "Mrs. Silverman? Is that you?"

"Eh? Who's there? Ach, David Shepherd...I should have known. It's nice to see you, dear." Gladys gave up trying to tug her cart up the one-step stoop of her entryway and laid her gloved hand to her chest. "I'm afraid this old heart is no longer as capable as it is ambitious."

"No problem. Let me get that for you." The cart was filled with groceries. "Been down to the market, I see."

"When you operate your own business, you shop when you can." She fumbled in the pocket of her black coat and brought out a whole handful of keys. "Here. Just a moment...I have it."

She unlocked the door with the sign in the window that read Closed. Try Again, and turned up the shop's brighter lights. Listening to the tinkling bell he couldn't see tacked to the door, David glanced around. As before he was a bit disconcerted with the strange little shop. There was a mannequin dressed much like Mrs. Silverman in the front window, a cedar lawn chair beside it and a dusty mauve armchair on its other side. Surrounding all that were dozens and dozens of "treasures"—tables with buttons and pins, medals and rings . . . walls filled with prints and paintings . . . coat racks with hats, military caps and scarves . . . and makeshift shelves of books, magazines, records and whatnot.

David had found Harmony's butterfly in one of the glass-topped cases, and from the way Gladys was watching him, she knew he was thinking about that again. There was a knowing, satisfied look on her face that disappeared the moment he asked about where she wanted the groceries.

"I hate to be a bother, but would it be too much trouble to bring them to the back? Through that way." She gestured to the curtained doorway when he glanced up the stairs.

"Ah, you think I live up there? No more. I use the efficiency apartment in back. I'm too old for stairs. Besides, what does one woman need with so much space?"

He wheeled the cart beyond the gold-and-copper damask draperies and into the smaller living quarters. To his surprise it was much neater than the store. Compact but charming.

His thoughts must have shown on his face because Gladys burst into soft laughter.

"You think because I collect other people's unwanted possessions I live in squalor, David?"

"No, ma'am."

"You're sweet. I think our beautiful Harmony could do a lot worse than you."

Ah, so now it would come. David drew in a deep breath to prepare himself. "About what you saw the other day, Mrs. Silverman—"

"Please? I saw nothing."

Her shrug was elaborate. Thinking about it and what she might have up her sleeve, he parked the cart by the kitchen table. "You know about the bad blood between the Martins and my family? You know what her family would say if they knew we were seeing each other. Well, trying to see each other."

Removing her knit gloves, she nodded. "Romance is stressful in times of hardship. Yes, I know, David. Once I was young, believe it or not. And quite a dish, if you'll excuse my immodesty. There was a boy, and like you and your Harmony it was difficult for us to even speak."

"What are you trying to say, Mrs. Silverman?"

"Only that I understand the problems you two are facing."

On the one hand he wanted to trust the woman, but on the other he couldn't help being suspicious. And if Mrs. Silverman was after something, David knew his first responsibility was to protect Harmony. "That's generous of you, Mrs. S. But I have to get back on the street."

"Of course you do. And I'm too tired to discuss things tonight."

"Things?"

"Yes, dear. Not to worry. Come back Friday."

"Why?" he asked, dazed. How had the conversation gotten out of control? "I mean—I work Friday, Mrs. Silverman."

"Before dinner or after? You do eat dinner, don't you?"

"Well, yes. And I'll be working the day shift Friday."

"Then come for supper. You can tell me what's on your mind then."

On *his* mind? "Mrs. Silverman, I don't think—"

"Friday, David. Now go. My bunions are killing me." She waved him out of her kitchen and back through the store.

At the front door she let him out and peered at him through the crack opening as he stood there staring at her. "Don't look so worried, dear. I'm the least of your problems."

David stood out in the freezing night and wondered.

Chapter Six

He'd planned to work a double shift Friday night, but Gladys Silverman's indeclinable invitation threw a hefty wrench into David's plans. Sure, he knew he could still manage the schedule. Maybe, if he could take an extended dinner. However, he had a feeling Mrs. Silverman had quite a bit to say. Heaven knows, he had a few things to get straight with her. As a result, he was hardly cheerful as he traded days off with the only other single man on the force. But he didn't tell his family. There was no way he could explain his schedule to them without raising questions. His mother was shaking her head over his absentmindedness more and more, and there weren't words to describe his youngest sister's watchful attitude toward him.

To escape all that, once he completed his day shift, he lingered at headquarters and resigned himself to trying to catch up on paperwork. But for the most part he kept watching the clock until it was time to head for Secondhand Treasures.

When it was time—actually, five minutes early—he drove with a heavy heart to Maple Street. Along the way he practiced what he wanted to say to her, and tried to prepare himself for what she might say to him. All he wanted out of this meeting was some reassurance that he and Harmony had a prayer of a chance to spend more time together, to solidify their bond before they told their families. It wouldn't happen if Gladys stuck her unwanted nose into their business.

He knew his mouth was compressed into a grim line as he arrived at the shop. Unsurprisingly there was the sign on the door announcing Closed. Try Again. The lady had more emergencies than Vermont had apple farms.

Hoping this one might be legitimate and that he could avoid their meeting altogether, he tried the doorknob. Unhappily it yielded.

He sighed.

The sleigh bell on the back of the door jingled. The scent of bayberry and amber tempted his nose. Then with a sweep and rustle as she brushed aside some crepe-ribbon garland hung around the damask curtaining, his hostess emerged from the back room.

"Hello! You're late."

"I'm early."

"Whatever." She shrugged and motioned with a tray filled with some variety of finger food. "Come this way."

Upstairs? He thought she'd said she didn't live up there any longer. And why was she all bundled up in her boa, felt and fur? As he followed her up the dark stairway he felt a momentary unease. The curse of a cop, he tried to tell himself, ever suspicious, even of eccentric little old ladies.

But as he approached the top of the stairs and noticed the flickering lights his internal alarm signaled again. Fire? No, candles.

Jeez, what was she up to?

As he reached the second floor he opened his mouth to make some excuse, announce an emergency of his own. Then he rounded the corner and saw—Harmony...standing in the middle of the room looking very trapped and nervous.

She gasped.

His heart felt as if it had just taken an injection of helium.

Despite her troubled expression, she looked lovely. He couldn't believe she was actually here. Wondering if he was dreaming this, he glanced at Gladys Silverman for an explanation.

"What? You're going to stand there like a block of wood? Come in. Make yourself to home. I was telling Harmony, only minutes ago I learned a friend of mine had been taken to the hospital. I have to go. But you two stay. Dinner is waiting in the oven. Enjoy. Talk. If I'm not back before you have to leave, just lock the door on your way out."

And with an almost girlish giggle she shuffled back down the stairs.

Still not confident that he'd figured this out, David turned to Harmony. "What's going on?"

"I don't know," she whispered.

"She told me I had to come, and I thought she was..." He decided he didn't want Harmony knowing how ungenerous he could be. "How did she get you over here?"

"Virtually the same way." Harmony's expression turned rueful. "Like you, I thought the worst of her."

He deserved that. "What do you think she's up to?"

"Matchmaking?" she asked with a shy shrug.

He thought she looked adorable, and wondered if they dared assume anyone would be so generous. It would make Gladys a certified fairy godmother, an angel in the flesh. But as he gazed at the woman before him, he decided he'd like to give the old lady any benefit of the doubt she wanted.

Harmony looked like a dream in her cranberry knit dress. It was modest, the hem just below the knee, but the gold buttons down the front picked up the fire in her eyes, and the suede belt emphasized her small waist.

"You look lovely. Thanks for wearing my pin."

Pleased, but also shy, she fingered the butterfly near her left shoulder. "It's become my favorite piece of jewelry."

Not wanting to ruin the mood, but needing to know, he asked, "Has anyone noticed at home?"

"Yes, and I was forced to lie. Just as I had to deceive them about how I got the scarf back." She looked away and bit her lip, clearly not proud of any of it. Then she noticed something else and she gestured to the counter. "Mrs. Silverman put out wine for us. Would you like a glass?"

He didn't need it. His head was already spinning with dreams about the possibilities of spending some stolen time with her. But she looked so eager to do something, anything, to occupy herself, he found himself murmuring, "Sure. Thanks."

Watching Harmony was a heady experience all its own. Her hair looked freshly washed and brushed to where it fell in heavy waves around her shoulders, as if she'd spent hours preparing for a date. Of course, common sense told him she'd been teaching all day and hadn't had time, but it was nice to pretend she'd gone through the trouble for him. Had she worn that outfit at school? He thought about all those teenage boys with their raging hormones who'd probably been visually devouring her from every angle, and experienced a twinge of compassion for the sweat that had probably broken out on their young brows, as well as a good deal of envy. No teacher of his had ever looked like her. She made his heart swell with pride and wrench with yearning.

"I think we were wrong, David," she said, handing him one of the long-stemmed goblets.

Her hands weren't quite steady and he had to fight the urge to take one and lift it to his lips for a reassuring kiss. But he knew she wasn't ready. He had to give her that time. "How so?" he murmured instead.

"We've been assuming the worst about Mrs. Silverman. But she's sweet. Very kind."

"I want to believe that."

"You can. Look at all this...what she's done for us. Isn't it obvious?"

He didn't feel like focusing on anything except *her*, but forced himself to take in their surroundings, and soon discovered she was right. Even as the aroma of something marinated drifted toward him from what looked to be an ancient oven, he saw the small table set by one of the windows. On an antique lace tablecloth that had to be big enough to be a bedspread was a glass dish of floating flowers—red silk carnations, but nice nonetheless—framed by white candles. It didn't matter that the candles were almost half gone, either, or that the silver-plate holders weren't a matched pair. It also didn't matter that at each place setting the china was slightly chipped or that the napkins were more of a Thanksgiving orange than a Christmas color. Maybe Gladys suffered from color blindness or something. All that mattered was that her heart was twenty-four-karat gold.

As he smiled at the single strand of Christmas lights in the window, multicolored and not perfectly hung but sweet, David decided that even the moon beyond it couldn't compete with it for romantic effect. He sighed. "She's really been planning, hasn't she?"

"I was speechless when I saw," Harmony whispered. "I still am."

"What did we do to bring this side out of her?" he asked, even as he thought of what she'd told him the other day about her sad past. Was it true, after all?

"I don't know...but isn't it lovely?"

He refocused on Harmony. "It's great that we're alone. But as for lovely—there's only one such sight in this room and you're it."

With a soft cry she stepped toward him, hesitated, uncertainty once again darkening her eyes. It was enough for David.

Putting down his glass, he was the one to close the distance between them, draw her into his arms. "Sweetheart..."

"David."

"Hold me. Put your arms around me. Hold me tight."

She did eagerly, her fingers clutching at the leather of his jacket. "It's so good to see you."

"That goes double, triple for me."

"I can't tell you how often I've wanted to call you."

"It's all right. I've felt it. I even called you."

She leaned back to stare up at him. "I didn't know."

"You couldn't. Besides, it was your grandmother who answered." As she gasped, he touched a hand to her lips. "It's all right. I hung up."

She immediately looked relieved and then guilty for letting him see that. "It's been hard."

"I know." That's why he wouldn't burden her with the full knowledge of how difficult it had been for him. All the thoughts that had been rambling through his mind since they'd last seen each other rushed through again and he had to hold Harmony closer to fight back the fears and doubts. "I've missed this. I've thought of little else. Except maybe figuring out how to see you again."

"It's been the same way for me."

"Really?" He knew he sounded like a lovesick teenager, but he didn't care.

"You wouldn't sound so pleased if you knew how hard I fought myself, David."

That put him back on level ground, put the steel back in his spine. "Are you still fighting? Do you want to leave?"

The way she looked at him nearly tore his heart in two. Pleasure and pain. Desire and fear. Hope and doubt. They were all there, and at his core he felt the punch and slice of each, as much as the caress and reassurance.

"I know I should."

He didn't like the lack of confidence he heard in her voice any better than he cared for what she said. "That's not what I asked." He cleared his throat, made his decision. "If we're going to play that game, I should go back to the station and tell them I can work the next shift after all. I should admit to you that there's nothing well-intentioned or conscientious about anything I'm thinking. I should get the hell down those stairs and out of your life."

"And why aren't you?"

"Because it's enough to stand here and soak in this moment for whatever it's worth. For as long as it lasts."

Harmony smiled. "That makes it easier for me to stay, David."

In other words she was looking to him to lead, but slowly; to decide, but carefully; to take, but tenderly. His problem was that he was tired of leading. No, not tired, he just wasn't sure anymore. When the heart got involved with right and wrong, everything seemed to get messed up.

"Take off your jacket," she murmured, picking up on his tension and doubt. "Your back feels as if it's ready to snap."

He did as she suggested. She helped and set it over the back of the couch, stroked her fingers over the soft material and did a slow turn. "I've been thinking that this feels almost surreal, something out of a forties romance. Even the furnishings play with your sense of reality. Mrs. Silverman says she rarely comes up here anymore. She says the stairs are too much for her. There's a bedroom, kitchenette and living room. And have you noticed this view? What more could anyone want?"

A king-size bed. Two weeks with you on a deserted island?

David had been trying to concentrate on what she'd been saying. Dutifully he nodded as she indicated the old but sturdy furnishings that followed no color scheme or style. He understood that as she was playing tour guide or hostess to him, she was getting her own emotions in control. Still, when she mentioned the view he was glad to have something to do. He picked up his glass again and joined her at the table to look outside.

Beyond the candlelight and the window decorations and a few young pine and hardwood trees, the nearly full moon illuminated the town lake, turning the water to liquid silver. David wished he could drive there with her. It was a favorite spot for lovers, and would-be lovers. But not them. Would they always be doomed to look at real life from a distance?

"Well, maybe it's not all that I thought," Harmony murmured when seconds passed and he remained silent. "Um, why don't you sit down, and I'll get our plates. She told me everything is already prepared and ready to be served."

He reached out and caught her hand. "I'm sorry. It's a nice view," he said gruffly.

"Sit," she whispered, and gently drew away from him.

The meal was some kind of chicken in a wine sauce with fresh potatoes and asparagus wrapped in something he had no intention of eating. As grateful as he was to their hostess, as hard as he tried to be enthusiastic, to make the proper responses when Harmony asked his opinion of everything, with each bite he could feel everything growing more and more strained.

He had no idea when she noticed. He *did* know she gave up trying herself after attempting to tackle the asparagus.

Suddenly she put her fork down and clasped her hands in her lap. "It's not working, is it?"

"It's fine." The chicken wasn't bad, just impossible to cut. "Great."

"Be honest. You're hating this."

Hearing something in her voice opened the floodgates for him. He set down his silverware, too. "I'm *hating* sitting over here when you're over there. We have such a limited time together, yet I'm trying to chase a quarter of a chicken around this platter. I hate—" He couldn't finish because of her crestfallen expression.

"She even made dessert," Harmony murmured, focusing on the base of the candle.

David couldn't take any more. He blew out the tiny flame then reached across the table and took her hand. "I don't want dessert. I want..." Feeling like a stuttering fool, he leaned over and pulled the plug on the window lights so that only the set by the window over the sink and the moon lit them. It was enough. Gazing at her in the soft glow, he stood and drew her to her feet.

"This is our first chance to be alone," he said, trying again, his voice low and urgent. "I don't want to spend it conforming to someone else's idea of a date. I feel we're beyond dates." He drew her to the couch. "We're at the stage of just needing to *be*. I want to learn what it's like to sit next to you," he continued as they settled on the firm cushions. "Really close. I want to find out what silence sounds like with you, and feel how our pulses become like one when your fingers are laced with mine.

"And I want to kiss you again," he added thickly, his gaze locking on her mouth. "God, I want that more than anything. Anything."

Unable to wait any longer, he brushed his lips against hers. When she sighed softly, he sucked in the faint sound, then deepened the kiss. Her reaction was gratifying—immediate and total acceptance. Reassured by the sweet invitation in her parted lips, certain his heart was thumping like a marauding bull elephant, he kissed her the way he'd kissed her at the park.

It was more powerful than before. Sitting without the armor of thick clothes, cocooned by the shadows, desire blossomed freely. *Feel me. Want me. Love me.* The emotions were acute, almost too much. And yet as they bathed David, he could feel a simultaneous effect on Harmony, and that she yielded with a poignant trust.

Wanting them to be linked in every way, he sought and joined their hands. The contrasts between them struck him anew, and he broke the kiss, as much to enjoy the sensations as to memorize the image of her elegant fingers entwined with his.

"So beautiful," he murmured, bestowing a kiss on her silky skin. "I still can't get over how these fine bones draw such powerful sounds from a chunk of wood."

Her answering laugh was whispery. "A very expensive chunk of wood."

"That reminds me." He discovered he liked kissing each finger separately, and then each joint. "Have you had any luck trying to get your violin repaired?"

Harmony sighed. "I sent it off the other day. It took me that long to get used to the idea that it may never sound the same again. It's so sad, David."

He drew her head against his chest, wanting to absorb her disappointment and worry. "Think positive. Maybe it will sound better."

She was still for a moment. Then, abruptly, she uttered an incredulous laugh and sat up. "Why haven't I thought of that before?"

"Because when people have been bombarded with too much change in their lives, as you and your family have, they fight hard to hold on to a status quo once things level off, even if that status quo isn't good for them in the long term. Everything has to change sooner or later, Harmony."

She studied him for a long moment, her expression tender, then traced the line of his strong jaw. "Philosophy, David?"

"Yeah," he replied with equal softness as he let himself dive deep, deeper into her bottomless eyes. "A cop with philosophy. Is that okay?"

She lowered her gaze to the badge, bright and uncompromising against his dark uniform. She fingered it as tentatively as if it were a living, venomous creature. He knew what was coming next, and when she shifted to touch his gun, he knew she understood.

"That can't change, sweetheart. I wish it could, but history remains the same no matter how hard we wish otherwise. What we can do is try to understand it clearly, though."

"Clearly?"

Breathing became a chore as his chest began feeling as if a band was tightening around it. He'd always known she didn't understand completely about that night twelve years ago, and now he saw that it was time to set the record straight. They had to if he and Harmony were to have a prayer of a chance.

He brushed her hair back over her shoulders and framed her face with his hands. "Something happened the night your father died that you need to know about, Harmony."

An icy dread filled Harmony. She didn't like what was happening, the alterations in David's demeanor, his forcing her to go back yet again to a time that still gave her nightmares.

"Whatever it is, I don't want to hear it," she told him, barely able to make her lips form the words. "Don't ask me to, David. I can't."

"You have to. For us."

"You're frightening me." Why was he ruining everything? She'd been reluctant to come here, and fear had underscored her joy once she'd seen him. Had she known it would come to this? No. She'd thought her only crisis would be if he wanted to make love to her. Would she have let him?

"I'm sorry, sweetheart." He sighed, drawing her close to his pounding heart. "The truth is I'm as scared as you are. I'm afraid that you won't listen. And I'm afraid that if you do you won't believe me."

"Would you lie to me?"

"No." His chest rose and fell on a heavy breath. "But what I have to say is going to be painful. You see . . . the night your father was held up at the nursery, it wasn't bad judgment on my uncle's part that got him killed."

Harmony jerked away. "Your uncle shot my father!"

"It's not that simple. It wasn't carelessness or bad judgment—it was an *accident*."

As David sat forward and tried to reach for her, she jumped up and stepped back, wrapping her arms around her waist. "Says who? Just because some board of inquiry believed him doesn't mean he told the truth. The arrested man said he lied. He said your uncle shouldn't have shot because he was using my father as a decoy!"

"You'd take a convicted felon's word over mine?"

She began shaking like a leaf, and figured she must have looked ready to drop because he hurried over to her and took hold of her by her upper arms. "Don't. I can't think when you're this close."

"Harmony, sweetheart, listen to me. I've heard Douglas tell us about that night in court, at home and a couple years later in a bar when he got so drunk he could barely stand. He tried to tell your mother, too, but she was in too much pain to listen."

"When? Where?" Harmony frowned. "I don't remember that."

"I'm not surprised. Your mother wanted to protect you. But Rod knows," he added, giving her a level look. "And he was there when your mother attacked my uncle and told him to get away from her and her family and never come back."

Harmony thought back and realized she must have been upstairs with her grandmother being held, and rocked, and sung to until she'd fallen asleep. Having lost her grandfather only a short time before, she'd walked around for days in a state of shock.

But that was then. Now she was older, stronger. She could take this, couldn't she? "What did he tell her?" she demanded flatly.

David shook his head, and at that moment Harmony almost believed this was as difficult for him as it was for her.

"Your father made a mistake. He lost it. Instead of letting my uncle handle the situation, he spotted a hammer and tried to go after the man himself. My uncle didn't see your father until it was too late. He stepped in front of that bullet, Harmony."

"No."

"Yes. Oh, God, sweetheart, the tragic part is that it was all perfectly understandable. Here was this hardworking, proud man . . . a man fed up with hearing and reading about thugs who preferred to rob and steal instead of earning like everyone else. He decided it wasn't going to happen in safe, rural Appleton. No one was going to take food from his babies' mouths."

"Stop it, David." Harmony clapped her hands over her ears. "You're telling me that my father was stupid!"

"No! Just too brave. Too quick to react. He didn't give the system a chance to work for him. Yes, sometimes it fails. But it wouldn't have that time, honey. Not during Douglas Shepherd's watch."

Harmony began shaking her head. "We never heard any of this."

"No one from your family was at the inquiry."

"The papers didn't mention it, either."

"What papers?" His disdain made him look older and harder. "The *Appleton Gazette?* The *County Trader?* They don't even employ reporters, let alone have people qualified to cover that sort of story, and you know it."

"I don't know anything!" Harmony cried, striking out at him, at the uniform, badge and gun that had cost her and her family so much. "I don't know any such damned thing! I only— Oh, God, David!"

There was no stopping the tears that had already soaked her cheeks. She'd believed she had finished crying for that tragedy years ago, had completed the mourning cycle. But as she reached for David as frantically as she'd struck out at him, she knew she'd been kidding herself.

"Shh... Come sit down. Come on, sweetheart. Have a seat and let it out. I know it's hard."

"All these years, David. It's too much. I can't bear it."

"It's done. It's done now. But we have to go on, Harmony. Do you believe that? Do you believe me?"

He'd led her back to the couch, his soothing words and tone a balm against the pain. She was most grateful, however, for his broad chest and pressed her cheek against it, seeking his strength. With him to lean on she could dare to look back and think clearly.

It would have been so much easier to continue believing that Douglas Shepherd had been careless. Overly ambitious. Instead she had to face the fact that her father had, for a split second, forgotten that he had a wife and four children at home who relied on him to be there, who would lose a part of themselves in losing him....

Damn it, Daddy.

"I wish I could carry your grief for you. I wish I could turn back the clock and give you those lost years." All the while he spoke, David stroked her hair, and in between he pressed soft kisses to her temple, brushed his cheek against hers. "You were given a gift to bring joy to people and it kills me to see you hurting."

Harmony opened her eyes, focused on the festively set table, the barely touched food. Mrs. Silverman's gift. She'd wanted to help them capture the spirit of their holiday—and she didn't even share their faith. Mrs. Silverman, a woman with her own share of tragedies. Yet she'd survived, and found her own reasons to smile and laugh. Maybe Gladys Silverman understood the spirit of Christmas better than any of them.

"Oh, David," she whispered, laying her hand over his badge. "I was wrong to have lashed out at you."

"It's all right."

"No. I tried to block out your words. Even now I'm not sure what I can accept. But..."

"Go on," he coaxed, his voice gruff. He lifted her chin and looked deep into her eyes. His own were filled with grief and stunning compassion. "Tell me."

"The only way any of this—us—makes any sense to me is when I focus on you." She studied his face, softened by the candlelight, but as always strong and handsome. "The first time I knew I felt something for you, you'd stopped to teach a child how to tie his shoe in the square. It was your rookie year. The child's hair was the same silvery gold as yours. I hadn't seen you in a while. You'd been in the air force and at college, and for a moment I thought you'd married, that he was yours."

"I don't remember that incident, but I wish I'd seen you." He stroked her cheek. "You've watched me, I've watched you. How is it that it took this long for us to connect?"

Blinking away the last of her tears, Harmony smiled and shrugged. "We're just dense, I guess."

"Then let's make sure we get this right," he murmured and closed his mouth over hers.

With a heartfelt moan she slipped her arms around his neck to draw him closer, parted her lips to him, needing to experience his tastes and heat again. The rest of the world might confuse and terrify her, but with David there was only peace and beauty.

His arms tightened and he lifted her closer. When that wasn't enough he drew her completely onto his lap. It was wonderful and reassuring to feel his power and protection. She leaned into it, gave herself up to him, to everything he would share with her. As his tongue swept along hers, tasted her, she couldn't hold back the soft mewing sound that rose in her throat. His hands moved restlessly over her back, into her hair, along her arms and to her hair again.

"I live for this," he whispered. "To have watched you play a concerto used to get me through the week, but now that I've held you, anything less is torture."

The next kiss was less tame and Harmony felt her body heat with a hunger too long dormant. Swept away in the tide of David's passion, she slipped her arms more fully around his neck to let him know she wanted to explore, was willing to venture into the territory he wanted to show her.

"Sweet, sweet heart."

Endearments ... caresses ... magic ... it spread a cocoon of warmth around her, made her feel special, beautiful. She tilted back her head and arched her neck as he skimmed kisses downward, downward. When he brushed his cheek against her breast, she felt it throughout her entire body.

"You're beautiful."

"You make me feel that way."

"I want to make you feel more." He backed away slightly to see her, to see what was in her eyes. "I want to make you feel everything." Like a fluid bow, he shifted again and planted a kiss in the lowermost point of her neckline. "Does that scare you?"

She understood what he was asking and she knew another crossroads was before them. Strangely enough, though, she had no second thoughts. Slowly taking his hand, she moved it to the first button on her dress. "Touch me."

Ever so gently, carefully, he eased her backward to the couch, then rose over her. A pillow fell to the floor, but neither of them cared. They had eyes only for each other. She watched him, focusing on his fingers slipping a gold-toned button free, then the one below it, and the one after that.

She was glad she wore her new black lingerie beneath the dress. It wasn't anything like the exotic inventions that were advertised in the mail-order catalogs she tried to peek at before Gran Irena used them to line the bottom of the trash bin for fear the twins would get hold of them. But she assumed David had already figured out that she didn't have a great deal of experience, and what's more that it thrilled him.

As his eyes darkened and his fingers hovered to part the dress farther, she came to understand the mystery and power of being a woman. And in that moment she knew that whatever she'd felt before for him, those emotions had just matured. Ripened. Wanting his mouth more than her next breath, she reached up to draw him down to her. His breath seared her breastbone, his lips whispered across the stark border of her slip before pausing to offer a nuzzling kiss to the inside swell of her left breast. The moistness, the heat nearly stole her breath, then his hand cupped her and she realized she hadn't begun to understand what her body craved.

As his thumb began to discover her shape and caress, she couldn't keep from moving restlessly beneath him, one moment curling to keep the sensations close, the next stretching to urge the eddying vibrations throughout her entire body. And David watched and coaxed and finally with a husky oath he rose over her and gave her the kiss of dreams.

With their hearts pounding as one, their legs entwined like the vines on a passion flower, David's talented hands slid into her hair and held her head as if in prayer.

"I want you."

"I'm not afraid."

He forced her to meet his somber stare. "No, you don't understand. I don't just want to make love with you, I want to marry you."

His words didn't register for a moment. She didn't let them. But like his gaze, the echo of his voice in her head was relentless.

Her silence had an understandable effect on him. He stiffened, sat up and drew her with him. "What's wrong?"

Wanting to smooth away his frown, to ease the grimness pulling at his firm mouth, she reached up to stroke and soothe. "David. Let's not ruin this."

"I said I want to marry you," he told her. "How am I ruining it?"

He'd never spoken to her more gravely, his gaze had never moved so restlessly over her face. It was as if he suddenly didn't recognize her. "I thought I'd explained everything. I thought you understood?"

"I do. I think. I mean, I'm trying," she amended, knowing she had to be completely honest with him. "But, David, that doesn't mean my family ever will. They'll never understand *us* wanting to be together."

He released her, moved off the couch as if he suddenly couldn't stand being so close. "You mean it's okay for me to have your body, but what we feel for each other isn't worth fighting for? Well, honey, thanks, but no thanks. That's just not good enough!"

Chapter Seven

How could he have said that to her? How could he have been so cruel? She'd wanted to share her love with him, she'd wanted to give him the greatest gift a woman can give a man—her trust—and he'd flung it all back at her.

She couldn't breathe. She couldn't think. All she knew was that she needed to get away.

"Wait a minute. Harmony—don't run!"

She didn't know she was until she was halfway down the stairs. Somehow she'd even managed to grab her coat and purse. Although she redid her buttons, she didn't pause to dress for the frigid night, just dug out her car keys and raced out of the building. As she flew down the street toward her car she suffered another spasm of guilt for all the work Mrs. Silverman had gone through for them, and for leaving behind a mess. Later she would apologize to the dear woman, try to explain. But right now all she wanted was to get home, lock herself in her room and try to forget the humiliation and the pain.

Her breath was coming in pants by the time she reached her car, and her cheeks felt on fire. In comparison, her poor vehicle resisted and protested against the bitter cold.

"Please."

As though it heard her, the engine coughed and sputtered, and sprang to life. Aware her brother would lecture until blue if he saw this, she ground the gears and hastily pulled away. Her headlights illuminated the front of Secondhand Treasures and she spotted David rushing outside. He yelled something she couldn't hear over the blowing heater and her chattering teeth, but there was no missing his wave of entreaty.

She stepped harder on the accelerator.

How she made it home, she had no idea. She knew she broke every speed limit between downtown and her house, but she doubted that she would have been able to stop even if she'd seen any flashing lights behind her. What she did note, however, as she pulled in to the driveway, was that Rod's truck was there.

Good grief, she wondered, what time was it? Just before she shut off the engine she checked the dashboard clock and bit her lip. They'd been at Mrs. Silverman's longer than she'd thought. It was minutes before ten. Of course Rod was back home; the store closed at nine during the holidays.

She had to pull herself together before she went inside. As unobservant as her family could often be about things that were important to *her,* she had a feeling that tonight they would only have to glance at her to know something was drastically wrong.

Grabbing her coat, she climbed out of the car and struggled to slip it on. Up and down the block Christmas lights twinkled merrily. Usually she loved to linger outside and enjoy the view, in the same way she liked to take different ways home to see how people on other streets had decorated. Tonight, however, it was all a blur, thanks to the tears that kept threatening to spill over. Well, it was cold enough to cry, she assured herself, heading for the sidewalk. Maybe she could convince her family of that if they said anything about the wetness that kept spilling onto her cheeks no matter how hard she tried to stop it. And she was known for being emotional, wasn't she? Sure, she could fool them.

The sound of screeching brakes, sudden acceleration and more brakes stopped her in her tracks. From up the road came the sharp lights of another vehicle racing recklessly down their road.

Her heart sank. It couldn't be, could it?

It was.

David spun crazily into the driveway and slammed to a stop. Harmony couldn't believe he could do anything so rash. And didn't he realize the noise would do more than attract her family's attention? She glanced around, certain that half the block was on their way to their doors and windows.

"Harmony—I need to talk to you!"

"Are you crazy?" She glanced back at her house, then back at him. "Go away, David. Before it's too late, go *away!*"

"No. What I said before...it was wrong. I was afraid. Hurt."

She didn't want him to come closer, but with long-legged strides he ate up the distance between them.

Before she could bring up her hands, he had hold of her arms. "If there's an ounce of compassion left in you, leave."

"Shepherd!"

The sound of Rod shouting David's name stopped Harmony's heart. She spun around in time to see her brother coming down the front stairs like a charging bull. Murder flared in his dark eyes.

Without hesitation Harmony stepped in his path. "Rod, this is none of your business."

"The hell it isn't." Rod took hold of her shoulders. "Get out of my way, Harmony. Better yet, you get inside."

She resisted his not ungentle push. "I won't."

"Harmony! Listen to him," her mother called from the front stoop. "Come here, dear. Rod will handle it."

She couldn't believe it. Now her mother and grandmother had joined in. There could be no hope of peace.

"See what you're doing?" Rod snapped at David. He moved around her and went toe-to-toe with him. "Not only are you upsetting my sister, but my mother and grandmother. What do you think you're doing here, anyway?"

"It's none of your business," David replied, though politely enough. "But I think it's fairly obvious. I'm here to see your sister."

Rod looked back over his shoulder at her. His gaze settled on her mouth and his eyes narrowed. Unable to stop herself, she lifted her fingers to her lips. She hadn't thought to check her lipstick, but it had to be gone. The kisses she'd shared with David all but guaranteed it.

With a guttural roar Rod swung back to David and, using his whole body weight, lunged at him.

"No!" Harmony screamed.

"Harmony, come up here this minute!" her mother commanded.

Although she knew she would have much to explain later, Harmony ignored her and tried to step between Rod and David again. "This is crazy. David, you have to get out of here."

"Not until I talk to you first."

"Can't you see she doesn't *want* to talk to you, Shepherd?" Again Rod outmaneuvered her and used the leverage to shove David. "Do you think your uniform and badge are going to protect you? That you can do whatever the heck you want?"

"If it's a fight you're trying to pick, Martin, you're wasting your time," David said, raising his hands to signal his refusal to be prodded. "You're not going to make me fight you."

"Wanna bet?"

Not in her wildest dreams did Harmony believe Rod would strike David. Seeing her brother's fist fly was horrifying. To see the blood on David's lip was a nightmare.

"No more!" she cried, grabbing and tugging at Rod's sweater. "Rod—I'm begging you—listen to me!"

As her brother tried to wrestle free of her hold, David spit blood. She couldn't deny her concern was mostly for him. Despite what he'd said tonight, her heart broke for him. "Go, David. Please. Haven't you had enough yet?"

She let Rod all but tug her into the house. Of course, her mother and grandmother took charge at the top of the porch. She wanted desperately to look back to see if David was all right, but before she could they had her inside.

"I'm calling the police," Gran Irena declared, a flash of black and silver that left her looking like one of the vengeful fairy-tale characters she had introduced Harmony to as a child. Life, death, bills, heartbreak...everything had always been handled in the kitchen. But for Harmony tonight the lights were too bright. There would be too many eyes, too, and too many questions without the law.

"No, Gran. You'll do no such thing." Harmony fought to keep her wits about her.

"*Cos 'e questo?* Little one, the man was stalking you. The authorities need to know that once again one of their own is guilty of betraying the public's confidence."

"He wasn't stalking me!" Hearing the shrill note in her voice and seeing her mother's and grandmother's startled expressions, Harmony all but fell into the chair they drew out for her. "We'd been together a few minutes before, okay?"

"Define 'before,'" her mother demanded, frowning.

She didn't see Rod enter the room. But the rude sound he made caught her attention.

"Can't you guess? Look at her. No lipstick, her hair a mess..." He swore, earning gasps from his mother and grandmother.

"We had dinner!" Harmony snapped. She refused to let him cheapen things, no matter what.

"For the love of heaven, why?" her mother gasped.

"I wanted to. David Shepherd was the officer on duty the night I was mugged."

Her mother took her coat and put it over the back of another chair. She was the only one who looked more concerned for her than indignant or offended. "That's no reason to feel obligated to have dinner with him. Harmony, your soft heart is going to be your undoing." As she rubbed Harmony's hands, she *tsk*ed again. "Mama, she's frozen through and through. Maybe you could pour from that pot of coffee we made when Rod got home. In fact, I think we all need something."

Harmony patted her mother's hand in gratitude, but shot a look of rebuke at her brother. "You were wrong to hit him."

"It's been coming to him for years, always looking and acting so self-righteous and sanctimonious as though *we* were the ones who owed *his* family an apology."

Every condescending word sliced at Harmony and she knew that no matter what it cost her, she couldn't remain silent. As her grandmother set out mugs and her mother poured coffee, she forced herself to say, "He told me something tonight that you'd better listen to. It's about Daddy. I didn't want to listen at first, but . . . I think maybe we've been acting too much like Rod."

"What?"

She faced her indignant brother. "You heard me. And it's time we stopped making excuses."

"There've been no excuses," her mother countered. "Harmony, you should be ashamed of yourself for suggesting such a thing. Your father was cut down in cold blood!"

"Murdered by your boyfriend's uncle!" Rod added.

"That's what we prefer to believe because it's safe and neat." She clasped her hands tightly, willing, praying for understanding. "But what if something else happened? What if there was a terrible, tragic accident, but an *accident* nonetheless?"

Her mother's still-beautiful face took on a haughtiness that would have intimidated someone ten years her senior. "Do you realize what you're suggesting, young lady?"

"This has been troubling David for years," Harmony answered, gesturing with appeal.

Her brother snorted. "He wants to whitewash his uncle's name."

"He doesn't have to. His uncle was cleared during the inquiry, remember?"

Rod glared. "Politics."

"Was it? He never considering running for chamber of commerce president like someone else I know," Harmony retorted. Then she bit her lip. "Rod, Mama. He told me... he told me that Daddy made a mistake that night. How he tried to take on something he wasn't qualified to handle." Briefly, gently, she told them the story.

"That's a lie!" Rod shouted, his dark eyes wild with fury and revenge.

Her mother uttered a cry and pressed her hand to her mouth.

Her grandmother crossed herself.

"Is it a lie, Rod?" Harmony challenged, despite her anguish. "Or is the memory you've built of Daddy the lie? Don't you think it's time we let him be human and fallible again? To deny him that isn't fair to him or us."

Rod jumped to his feet. "I'm not listening to another word of this...this garbage. Maybe you can buy into what your boyfriend is selling, but not me!"

"I'm so disappointed in you, Harmony," her mother added. "None of us deserve this, most of all your father."

"I'm disappointed in *you,* Mama. I loved my father, but I would never ask my children to blame the past on the innocent the way you've taught us to shun the Shepherds. Now I don't know if what David's uncle told him was the truth or not. None of us will ever be able to prove anything one way or another. But I do know I'm tired of living in ignorance and hate. It's diminishing us, Mama!"

All three of them stared at her. The room reverberated with her words and their silence. And in that silence Harmony felt their censure. She was only glad that the twins didn't have to experience this. They'd been only babies when they'd lost their father. In a way that had been easier; they'd never learned to miss who they'd lost.

"I cannot deal with this. I'm going to my room to lie down," her mother said at last. She rushed out and, muttering some Italian homily Harmony only half understood, her grandmother followed.

Alone with her brother, she waited. Rod wasted no time in making his feelings known.

Leaning toward her, he whispered, "Never do anything like that to Mom again. And stay away from Shepherd."

"Don't threaten me, Rod."

"Don't push me, little sister."

"David, merciful heaven. What happened?"

He knew he had to look pretty bad because he *felt*

like hell, but one glance at his mother's and father's horrified expressions and he realized it had to be worse than anticipated. Easing the door shut behind him, he winced as he tried to shrug out of his coat. Although he hadn't hit the ground very hard, thanks to the snow piled alongside the Martins' walk, everything ached. But it wouldn't do to let his parents know how much.

"I'm okay," he murmured, trying to baby his swollen lower lip.

"You are not!" His mother rushed to help him, and tossed his jacket onto the couch. She then framed his face in her hands to hold him still for a closer inspection. Almost as petite as Harmony, but far stronger, she had no problem in keeping him still. "Honey, did this happen on the job?"

He wished. "Not exactly."

"It must have if you're home this early."

"No. I didn't work tonight." But he wasn't about to go into *that* with them.

"I'll get you a washcloth and an ice pack. Glenn, dear, maybe you'd better get him a shot of whiskey. It will help kill any germs around that cut. He looks like he could use the boost, too."

Despite her tendency to coddle, his mother was all right—virtually overrunning the household and her daughters, still she understood the male psyche and ego. That's why when his sister Shawna wandered in from the kitchen with a bowl of popcorn and hooted and pointed at him, his mother took hold of her bathrobe belt and tugged her back into the kitchen.

"Your mom's right. Sit down, son, and I'll get it for you." Looking rattled for a man with considerable law-enforcement experience himself, his father hurried to the antique buffet they used as a bar.

David took everyone's absence as an opportunity to peer into the ornately framed mirror over the couch. Hell, he thought, and would have grimaced if it hadn't hurt so much. But the throbbing and stinging was nothing compared to the rest of his pain. He felt as if he were bleeding internally.

God, if only he hadn't reacted like a jerk when Harmony had panicked. He should have expected her to get cold feet; he'd given her a big shock when he'd told her about her father. To add a proposal on top of that... Stupid, stupid, stupid. But he was in love and there'd been no stopping him. His mouth had outrun his brain.

He slumped onto the couch and buried his face in his hands. Okay, so he hadn't exactly proposed. He'd only made his intentions known. But that was enough. Worse.

So much for planning, for buying her a ring, taking her somewhere elaborate for a fancy dinner... all the stuff a woman waited for when she got engaged. All that he wanted to do for Harmony to show her that this wasn't nearly as impulsive a thing as she might think. Instead he'd behaved thoughtlessly, clumsily. And there was no telling what Mrs. Silverman was going to say.

The firm grip on his shoulder told him his father was back with his drink. "Thanks."

The whiskey burned like the devil, but at least that was a change from the throbbing. David gasped, blinked and nodded to his father. "That should do it."

His father returned to his recliner facing the TV and used the remote control to shut off the set. "So what happened?"

"Rod Martin. He wanted to fight. I didn't."

As expected, his father scowled. "Where'd you run into him? Did they have a problem at the garden center?"

"No, it happened at their house. I was following Harmony."

"Whatever for?" His mother rushed back into the room with Shawna, minus the popcorn and looking dutifully penitent. "Were there complications with that incident at Revell's?"

"Uh-uh," he grunted, dabbing the washcloth to his chin and lip. Even the soft cotton made him wince.

"Were you going to ticket her for speeding?"

He took a deep breath. They had to hear sooner or later, he reasoned. As his mother settled beside him and he exchanged the washcloth for the ice pack, he murmured, "We're seeing each other."

Shawna shrieked and threw herself into the other recliner, rocking back to kick up her feet. "I told you! I told you!"

"Knock it off," her father snapped, and still scowling he turned back to David. "Is this some kind of joke?"

"Don't, Dad. She's beautiful, talented, intelligent—"

"She's a *Martin*," his mother interjected.

"I know!"

Looking at him as if he were an impostor, she shifted to the far end of the couch and crossed her arms. "How long has this been going on?"

How long, indeed. What would they say if he told them since the funeral? No, they wouldn't be able to handle that. He settled, instead, for a vague gesture of his free hand.

"Is it serious?" his father demanded.

"Of course it's serious, Glenn," his mother countered from her side of the coffee table. "When a man bleeds for a woman it's generally serious."

"Well, did he ever think what this would do to Douglas?" he demanded.

Watching smugly, Shawna tossed in, "Surely you saw it coming? The changes in him have been going on for months."

"Months." Her mother's expression matched that of an abandoned puppy he'd once found roaming the streets. "This is the last thing I expected of you, David. Harmony Martin..."

He shut his eyes and shook his head. "Don't. Don't start with the emotional manipulations. I've known I've wanted Harmony for a number of years. I'm not ashamed of it."

"We'll see what you say when your uncle gets wind of this," his father muttered.

"Well, damn it, here." David picked up the phone and slammed it onto the coffee table. "Call him! Do you think that's going to change anything? Do you think we asked for this? We didn't. We tried to ignore it, and when that didn't do any good, we fought it. And that's not doing any good, either." Now oblivious to the external pain, caught up in his inner agony, he rose from the couch and began pacing around the room.

"I knew I couldn't pretend not to care the night those two animals attacked her," he said, his voice deepening. "I look at what you and Mom have built for yourselves, the relationship you two have, and I want that for myself."

"But, darling, there are so many other girls who would jump at the chance to go out with you if you'd only *ask* them," his mother said more calmly.

"I'm not interested in anyone else, Mom. I love Harmony... and she loves me." She may not be able to admit it right now, but he believed it. He had to.

"She's said this?" his father demanded.

He paused, sensitive to what an actual admission would do to this conversation. "Under the circumstances some things don't need to be said. Besides, the situations's painful considering that we know what we're up against with our families."

His father slapped the arms of his chair with glee. "Did you hear that, Barb? There's hope. They appreciate the fact that we'd never approve."

David rubbed at his forehead. "Dad, I didn't say we would bow to any pressure one way or another." At least, *he* wouldn't, and he would do anything in his power to make sure Harmony didn't, either.

"Are you giving us an ultimatum?" his father asked, frowning again.

How could he do that when he didn't even know how long it would take to get Harmony to talk to him again? The one hope he had was remembering her expression when he'd left her. He would hold on to that for as long as necessary. "No," he murmured, "it's not an ultimatum, Dad. It's a promise."

Shawna gasped.

His mother leapt up from the couch as though someone had wired her cushion.

His father stared openmouthed.

"Uh, David, your lip," his mother began, the first to recover. "It's bleeding again and you'll get it on your uniform. Here, dear. And try to calm down."

"I've never been more calm."

"I believe it." His father's eyes grew flinty. "You must have been practically asleep to let Rod Martin hit you!"

"Glenn, that's not going to get us anywhere."

David signaled his mother not to bother. "What did you want me to do, Dad? Knock him out while I was in uniform so he could press assault charges? Get myself put on probation? Get my name in the paper? After what I told Harmony tonight, that would really go over well with her family. Not only would they never believe her, any confidence she'd had in what I told her would be over, too."

"What you told her?" His mother bit her lip. "Oh, David. You explained about her father?"

Shawna whistled softly. "How did Harmony take it?"

"How do you think? For twelve years she's lived with something that would be hard for anyone to handle. Now she hears that her father might not have had to die."

"Might?" His father snorted. "You're starting to sound more like a Martin than a Shepherd, boy."

"I was talking from Harmony's perspective," David explained wearily. He eyed the bloody washcloth and wondered how much more he could take. His head was beginning to pound. "Look..." One by one he met his family's wary, stunned, disappointed gazes. "I'm sorry this is hitting you when Toni, Lea, Jolene and the others are about to arrive and we were all looking forward to a great visit. I don't want to hurt you, and I've spent my whole life trying to make you proud of me."

"David," his mother cried, gripping his arm with reassurance. "There's never been any question of that."

He looked back at his father. "Then don't make me choose between you."

Chapter Eight

Convinced that the longer he waited the worse it would be, David tried to phone Harmony on Monday. As soon as he got to the station he dialed the school's number in the hope of catching her between classes. Not only did he fail and end up having to deal with the administration office, but they asked for his name and number, saying they would have her return the call. Knowing she wouldn't once she saw the message they would hand her, and that she also wouldn't appreciate the questions his calling would raise in administration, he made an excuse and said he would try again later.

Thwarted but not checked, he settled for driving slowly past the school to look for her in the windows. But either her class was on the opposite side of the school or hers was the series of windows where the blinds were lowered.

Still determined, he planned to try to corner her later as she made her way to her car, but minutes before heading toward that side of town again, he was called to intervene in a fistfight that had developed after a fender bender. Wondering about people's sudden predilection for using brawn instead of brainpower, he dutifully changed course for the fracas across town.

It was much later, when he was between shifts and lingering at the station, that he decided he had nothing to lose. He tried calling her at home.

A young male answered on the first ring. "Yeah?" he shouted above the loud music in the background.

Heaven save us from portable stereos, David prayed silently. "Harmony Martin, please."

"Just a second. *Harmony!*"

Grimacing as he held the phone away from his ear, he thought the kid—probably one of the twins—could put a bull elephant to shame. He wondered how a family as stiff-necked and tunnel-visioned as the Martins handled hard rock reverberating through the house.

Unfair, Shepherd. Now who's holding on to old bitterness?

Hoping that the teen and his sister were the only two at home, he heard the telling click that indicated the extension was finally picked up.

"I have it, Brandon—and please turn that thing down before the plaster cracks!"

The voice was female, but he couldn't determine anything else with all the interference. "Harmony?"

She paused, then demanded, "Who's this, please?"

His heart sank. The kid had finally hung up and he could now tell the woman's voice was older, a bit sharper than he'd first realized. His hunch was that instead of Harmony, he'd gotten hold of her mother. He swore silently. How long before his luck changed?

"Excuse me, ma'am. Is Harmony there, please?"

She, too, hesitated and then snapped, "No, she is not, and even if she was, I wouldn't let you speak to her. Stay away from my daughter, do you hear me? She wants nothing to do with you!"

His ear ringing from the sound of the slamming receiver, David ran his tongue over his still-sore lip and tried not to buy into the woman's attempt at stonewalling him. Harmony *did* want to see him, he had to continue believing that. She was just letting her feelings for her family override her feelings for him. He hoped.

But his luck didn't improve the next day, or the next, no matter where or what he tried. He began to believe that maybe fate was conspiring against him. He didn't, however, let his disappointment and dejection stop him from getting over to Secondhand Treasures.

At first Gladys Silverman looked as if she wanted to throttle him. But when she spotted the blooming Christmas cactus he'd brought as a peace offering, along with a cake from the bakery in town, she deigned to forgive him.

Stepping from behind the counter, she wrapped her zebra-print sweater tighter around her plump middle and beckoned. "Come in the back. You can put all that beside the roses Harmony brought me."

"Harmony was here?" David asked, brightening. "When?"

She held back the curtain for him. "A day before yesterday, Mr. Slowpoke. What's in the box?"

"Cheesecake. I thought we could have coffee together."

She brightened considerably. "Maybe you're a good boy, after all, David Shepherd. But you could have called me that night to let me know if you two were all right," she said, pinching his arm through his jacket. "I knew there was something wrong. Not because you two ate like birds or barely touched the wine, but because you knocked one of my pictures off a wall as you slammed the door on your way out."

"Jeez, I'm really sorry," David said again, feeling terrible for that, as well. "Did it break? Let me pay for it."

As he reached for his wallet she waved him away. "Forget it. It was an ugly picture and an uglier frame. I was glad to be rid of it."

"Well, I am sorry," he said, surprised at how much he meant it. He was deeply indebted to this strange old woman. She'd given them a chance when no one else had. "I wouldn't blame you if you never spoke to me again."

"Hmph," she replied with a toss of her head that made her reindeer earrings do a jig. "How am I going to learn any gossip if I do that? Sit. Tell me what went wrong."

Feeling somewhat sheepish, he set the cake on the kitchen table and the plant where she'd directed, on the wrought-iron stand by the window. Harmony's roses were a rich, romantic red, almost the color of the dress she'd worn the other night. "Didn't she explain?" he asked, aching inside.

"Of course." Water ran and pots clattered. "But that doesn't mean I don't want to hear your version."

He kept it brief and the old woman pouted.

"You're as stingy with details as she was. Tell me this, then—it's good between you? The feelings are there? You feel she cares the same as you?"

Confident of little else, he nodded. "She's afraid to admit it, but . . . I think so. Maybe you should tell me. I haven't gotten her to talk to me since I won this fat lip from her brother."

"Feuding families," she droned, setting two mismatched mugs on the counter and taking a jar of instant coffee from the refrigerator. "They'll drain the sweetness out of romance, my boy. They'll make you feel guilty for daring to love, or not loving who they want you to love, or... Ach, it's no good." She waved her hand dismissively again. "You know what your problem is? You've both lived with your family for too long. You've become as comfortable as old shoes to them, and that," she added, wagging a gnarled finger, "creates trouble. You should move out on your own. It's the only way they'll wake up and realize their old roles are over."

"But we both have a deep sense of commitment to our families. You know our backgrounds, the story about my uncle and Harmony's father. That's put certain obligations on us."

"Phooey. Who doesn't have tragedies or obligations in their life? Listen to me." Warming to her subject, she crossed to him and gripped his forearm with both hands. "You are a grown man, she is a grown woman. Go live your lives. The families will get used to the idea."

"And if they don't?"

"Then it's their loss."

He couldn't deny that most of what she'd said sounded reasonable. "But this is Appleton, Mrs. S.

We're not exactly experiencing a building boom here and I've heard finding suitable housing is difficult."

"You want a place?" She raised her hand, palm upward to the ceiling. "It's yours. Pay me what you can afford. Money means nothing to me, and I know that Harmony helps her mother financially. Me, I have more than enough."

David shook his head. "You're terrific, you know that?"

"Prove it. Talk to that girl of yours. You have a ring yet?"

If he'd been eating or drinking already, David would have choked. "Mrs. Silverman, I can't even get her on the phone!"

The old woman's false eyelashes collided with her eyebrows as she rolled her eyes. "Ei-yei-yei. I like you very much, David Shepherd. But I can see I need to teach you a few things about women."

Harmony had thought she understood misery. After six days of trying to keep peace in her family by avoiding David, she discovered she'd underestimated its power. And she didn't know how much more she could take.

With a clearer perspective of their evening together, she knew now that she hadn't been fair to him, let alone honest. It still embarrassed her to remember how she'd offered herself, asked him to share all his passion with her, only to turn coward the minute he asked for something in return. Granted, she'd been emotionally jarred by the revelation about her father, but she couldn't hide completely behind that excuse.

Yes, the story was tragic and sad, but even if David's uncle had been guilty of being careless, she knew it wouldn't have changed anything. David was in her heart, and he would always be there. The question was could she stand her family's censure if she went against their wishes and saw him again?

"Do you have a minute?"

She'd thought she was nicely tucked away in the school's practice room, safe from every interruption. But glancing up from the catalog she was studying for next year's band music, she was confused, not annoyed, because it was Paula and not a student who'd found her.

But at this hour? she wondered, glancing at her watch. Her friend had lunch-room duty this week and should have been there by now. "Something wrong?"

"That depends on how you look at things."

"Okay, I'll bite, but aren't you supposed to be keeping law and order, not to mention blueberry pie off the ceiling of the lunch room?"

"I was on my way, but I was coaxed off course by a certain gentleman in blue."

She'd never been good with guessing games and had always been a wallflower at parties where they were played. But Harmony had no difficulty in figuring out her friend's clue. "David . . . he's here?"

"Trying to look as inconspicuous as an officer of the law can appear in a school hallway at high noon with a few hundred curious teens staring at him with everything from male resentment to female lust."

Despite her surprise and concern, Harmony managed a wry smile. "I can imagine." Particularly the girls' reactions. But the smile quickly died. "Is he here to see me?"

Paula offered a needless pat to the nape of her short hairdo. "Well, my dear, try as I did to dazzle him with my not-so-innocent cat's eyes, he remained unimpressed. Since I saw the way you reacted to each other a few weeks ago, I took an educated guess and said I'd track you down for him."

Already out of her chair, she urged her friend back out the door. "Where do I go?"

"Side entrance. Are you going to fill me in on what's going on?" Paula added in a loud whisper. "He looks as miserable as you do."

Harmony was grateful that her friend hadn't pressed her for information sooner. Paula had always understood that she wasn't the type who needed to talk out all her troubles with someone. But this time she thought it might help to have another woman's perspective. "I will. As soon as I can."

The side entrance was somewhat less busy than the front and back doorways, and Harmony was grateful David had chosen it. She spotted him as soon as she rounded the corner, and drew in a quick breath.

He looked good, so good. His lip was better, almost healed, and as always the police uniform enhanced his tall, strong body and blond good looks. Just the sight of him sharply silhouetted against the window made her heart race. When she got closer and saw his expression soften, his firm mouth curl into a tender smile, she had to slip her hands into the pockets of her jumper to keep from throwing herself at him.

"David." She glanced over her shoulder. "What are you doing here?"

"I won't stay more than a minute. I just had to see you." His gaze roamed over her face with barely concealed hunger. "Are you all right?"

"Yes. You?"

"No."

Alarmed, she stepped closer, gave in to the irrepressible urge to touch his chest and feel his heartbeat. "What's wrong?"

"What's not wrong? I haven't seen you in days. Haven't been able to touch you... your hair..."

Footsteps sounded. Harmony touched a finger to David's lips to silence him, but the heavy thump of a door opening and closing told her that the person had detoured and that they were still safe.

Before she could withdraw, David took her hand and kissed her fingertips, then moved to her palm, and in that kiss he managed to remind her of every intimacy they'd shared that night in Gladys Silverman's apartment. His clear gray eyes asked her if she was going to try to deny it, and what shimmered between them.

"But we can't talk here," she whispered.

"Will you meet me after school?"

"Where?"

He suggested the roadside park outside town again, then vetoed the idea. "If something happens and I get held up, I hate the thought of you being out there alone. There is another option." He told her about Gladys's standing invitation to use the apartment over her shop. "But if it reminds you of things you'd rather forget..."

"Only that I was unfair to you."

Hope and desire flared in his eyes and for a moment she thought he would ignore the need for discretion and sweep her into his arms. If he kissed her now, she knew she wouldn't be able to get through the rest of her classes. As it was, she knew her concentration would be shot for the day.

"I can be there by four," she told him.

"Great. I can arrange to take a break then. We won't have very long," he added, looking pained.

"I understand." She bit her lip, unable to help feeling guilty. "I have to get home, anyway. They're being very protective these days."

"I was afraid of that. Until four, then."

He looked as though he would leave, and actually made a step backward toward the door. But then his eyes settled on the butterfly pin. She wore it only at school, and had to be careful to remember to take it off before arriving at the house.

His throat worked, his chest rose and fell. Finally, with a soft oath, he shot forward and pressed his mouth to hers for one brief but stunning kiss. "Until four," he murmured against her lips.

He could barely stand the waiting. It helped to walk his beat through town, to stop and chat with the various merchants. The chief was fairly lenient about what his officers did during their shifts as long as they were visible, and he usually volunteered for foot patrol when whoever else on duty preferred to drive the perimeters of town. Today, however, he'd had to specifically ask for foot patrol in order to assure his presence at Mrs. Silverman's later. Fortunately, Clancy was still recovering from the flu and didn't mind being in a heated car at all.

The rendezvous was already arranged with their fairy godmother and when he arrived seconds before four and saw that Harmony's car was already parked in front of Secondhand Treasures, he nearly swung off the leather belt of sleigh bells Mrs. Silverman had recently added to the door.

"Ah, good afternoon, Officer Shepherd," the woman sang from behind the counter. She beamed and nodded as she paused in wrapping something in newspaper for a male customer whose attire suggested he shopped here regularly. "Nice of you to take time out of your busy day to help a frail old woman. The, er, boxes I mentioned needed moving are right up the stairs. Just put everything in the back room. But do me a favor, dear, shut the door while you're working so you don't disrupt the customers."

Her current customer was leaning unsteadily over the counter as if trying to read her lips. David guessed the old-timer had lost his hearing sometime between Truman and panty hose, but, grateful for what his benefactress was hinting at, he nodded. "Be happy to, Mrs. S. Won't take but a few minutes."

"Oh, darling, don't rush on my account. I would hate to be responsible for you hurting yourself."

With a dry smile, David set off. It might have looked slightly suspicious to take the stairs two at a time, but he didn't care. A bit winded when he reached the top, although more from excitement than racing, he had to do nearly a 180-degree turn before he found Harmony.

She stood flush against the stairway wall, a little anxious, but oh, so lovely. Earlier when he'd seen her, he'd thought her black jumper and white shirt with its Victorian collar sweet and youthful. But now he amended that to romantic. She looked like a heroine in one of the Daphne du Maurier books Toni had coaxed him to read ages ago.

Pausing only long enough to shut the door as Mrs. Silverman had directed, he extended his arms. She flew to him.

"Sweetheart," he breathed, emotion rocking him to his core. Too hungry to wait, he sought and found her mouth with his. A groan of relief and pleasure rose from deep in his chest as her warmth and softness seeped into him. Her name was a song that raced through his veins until there was nothing else for him but this woman.

Like him, Harmony didn't seem content with one long kiss or just holding him. The energy between them reverberated too powerfully, and it was a relief to indulge in fleeting kisses and restless caresses. Several times her hands collided with his as they renewed their knowledge of every muscle and curve and curl.

"I thought I'd lost you," he rasped, lingering with her hair, stroking her cheeks, kissing her forehead, nose and chin.

"Don't ever think that. Oh—your lip!" Horrified, she stared at where she'd just lightly bitten him. "Am I hurting you?"

"Only when you stop."

With a relieved laugh that ended in a moan, she buried her face against his shoulder. "It shouldn't have happened, David. He wouldn't have hit you if I hadn't run out of here like a selfish, imma-ture...coward."

"You aren't anything of the kind. And it was my choice not to fight him. Believe me, Rod and I could be in far worse shape right now."

She hugged him tight. "Thank you for protecting my brother. He doesn't understand, but I do. I truly do, David."

David closed his eyes for a moment and sent up a prayer of gratitude for this gift. But it was only sec-onds before he felt compelled to kiss her again. "How bad is it at home?" he murmured between reverent caresses.

Her sigh was telling. "I'm not under house arrest or anything, but they keep close track of where I'm going and when to expect me back. And my mother acts stiff and formal around me. As for my grandmother, she's suddenly begun retelling every story she can remember about my father, or else lecturing about moral values and allegiance."

"Sounds like dinner is a rollicking time at your house," David drawled, his smile compassionate. Stroking her back, he added, "What about Rod?"

She groaned. "He's the most upset. You see, when my father died, he assumed his role, and in a way he sees himself as my parent. As far as he's concerned, he's failed me. He sees me as sleeping with the enemy."

"I wish you were," David groaned, pressing a kiss to her forehead.

She leaned back to look up at him. "How long do we have?"

They were holding each other too tight for David not to know that she was as aroused as he was. "Not long enough. Ten minutes maximum."

Harmony made a sexy, yet pained sound. "I hate this. We've done nothing wrong." Once again she gazed up at him sadly. "I tried to tell them. About my father."

"Ah, sweetheart, I wish I could have been with you. You shouldn't have had to do it alone."

"It was difficult. But I understand why they became so angry. When my father died we lost a great part of our lives, too, a great part of our identity. The only thing that eased the hurt was anger. The angrier we grew, the easier we could cope.''

"All I need to know is if you believe what I told you?'' David asked, knowing what they felt for each other didn't have a prayer if she didn't.

"I didn't want to at first.'' Shadows of self-censure and disappointment darkened her eyes to nearly black. ''So many things were coming at me at once. All I had to hang on to was knowing how I felt when I was with you. But the last few days have given me a considerable amount of time to analyze and reflect, and...yes, I believe you.''

He felt a huge weight lifting off his shoulders. ''Are you sure? Don't say that because you think I need to hear it, or because you're trying to convince yourself.''

"David, when I looked back, I finally peeled away the halo we'd constructed around my father. Memories are tricky things when you're feeling vulnerable. They're the first thing you protect to ease the hurt. But once I forced myself to see honestly, I recognized things, the potential for my father to have reacted the way your uncle reported. He'd actually wanted to be a policeman, you know.''

"Your father? You're kidding?''

"No, it's true. Of course, the family's probably managed to forget that. I must have been about eight or nine, and I'd gone into the attic. I was looking for one of my grandmother's old dresses for a school play. In one trunk I found letters, pictures and other memorabilia, including his senior yearbook. Under his picture they listed law enforcement or journalism as his goal.''

"Instead he bought a nearly bankrupt nursery and became Appleton's professor of Plantae."

Harmony smiled. "He was rather good at it, wasn't he? But I remember he'd always have a comment about something in the newspaper, and whenever there was an argument in the neighborhood, he was the one who dove into the middle to stop it. My mother would get furious with him. Sometimes he'd even get a bruise or two himself." She shook her head. "I think he fooled my mother, but I don't think owning a nursery and understanding plants was enough for him. It's so sad. But recalling those episodes made me realize how easy it could have been for him to make a bad decision that night."

David laid his cheek against the top of her head. "Thank you for that."

"No. Thank you."

"What for? Shattering all your memories?"

"No, for not giving up on me. For having the patience to give me time to work it out for myself. For not hating me all those years when I avoided you and held a prejudice against you for being a Shepherd, the way my family did."

"The question is, are we going to continue letting them dictate to us?"

Her fingers bit into his jacket. "I won't let you down again, David."

He'd thought himself in love, but in that instant he knew he was just beginning to understand how much he cared. And this time, he vowed to himself, there would be no mistakes. "Do you realize what you're saying?"

"Remember who you're talking to," she replied with a soft sound that was part sob and part laugh.

With her next breath, however, she grew confident again. "All I know is that I don't want us to be apart any longer. David, not even my music can fill the loneliness when you're not with me."

He'd never heard anything half so sweet. "And I want to be with you more than these stolen minutes. I don't want to have to sneak around or have to hide what I feel. I meant what I said the other day. I want to spend the rest of my life with you."

As he reached into his pocket he realized his hand was unsteady and rather damp, but his fingers closed surely around the blue velvet box he'd been keeping close since he'd made his purchase last night after quite an earful from Mrs. Silverman. He drew it out and uncurled his fingers; watched her face as he opened the lid and held the box before her.

The ring wasn't elaborate by any means, the solitaire-cut stone hardly a blinding size, the gold band slender and simple. But he'd chosen it because he'd long noted that Harmony wasn't a woman to wear big, flashy jewelry. She didn't need to. His choice for her was like the butterfly pin—fine and understated, genuine like the woman he hoped would wear it.

"Oh. Oh, my," she whispered, pressing a hand to her heart. "David, this is..."

When she didn't finish, he felt an instant of anxiety. "You can't be surprised. When a man asks a woman to be his wife, it's expected that he be prepared."

"You mean you had it the other night?"

He wouldn't lie, although he would rather forget. "Er, no. *That* proposal caught me by surprise as much as it did you. Not that I meant it any less than I do now," he added quickly. "But let's just say I've had

time to, uh, think about things, and I realize how...
inattentive I'd been to certain details." Thinking
briefly about Gladys's long lecture, he almost smiled.
"You won't catch me stumbling again." No, not when
they had a fairy godmother who moonlighted as a
protocol expert.

Harmony simply continued to stare, mesmerized.

"Sweetheart?" David ducked his head. Despite his
nerves he was bemused by her expression.

"It's the most beautiful ring I've ever seen, David," she murmured slowly, as if dazed. A discreet
cough from the foot of the stairs snapped her back to
awareness. "Oh, Lord. You have to leave, don't
you?"

He shook his head, his mood resolute. "I'm not
going anywhere until I get my answer." Filled with a
new and empowering confidence, he slid the ring from
its slot and held it out to her. "Will you marry me,
Harmony Martin?"

Chapter Nine

The car drove itself home. It must have, because she spent the entire time staring at the sparkling ring on her left hand.

Engaged. Her... Harmony Aniella Martin... Mrs. David Jason Shepherd. It felt so unreal and yet romantic. No, it felt right.

"Aniella. That's beautiful. Is it Italian?"

"Mmm. It's from the word for lamb. Oh, my goodness! David—do you realize... ?"

Harmony smiled again as she thought of how the aptness of their names had struck them. The shepherd and the lamb, indeed. How wonderful it had been to laugh. How exciting it had felt afterward to hold up her hand and watch him slip on the ring. How amazed she'd been that the fit was perfect.

So was the kiss that had sealed the moment and their promise. Her body went hot and weak all over again as she remembered it. Something new had happened with this kiss, a maturity that underscored the beauty of what promises meant. Her heart ached as she recalled how they'd drawn out the moment, and how they'd resisted yielding to the demands time, his job, made on them.

The biggest question of all remained, though. How was she going to tell her family?

"Do you want me to come with you?"

"No, David. I love that you've offered, but this is something I have to do alone, just as you have to tell your family by yourself. We owe them that time alone with us."

"They'll try to talk you out of this. They'll try to convince you to give me back this ring."

"Yes, but they won't succeed. I promise."

But as she pulled in to the driveway and spotted Rod's pickup, her confidence suffered a major setback. She'd hoped to have some time alone with her mother and grandmother first. Rod had a tendency to make them more militant. Without his influence they could still be tough, resolute, but they were less quick to make explosive accusations and threats.

Well, she would just have to cope, she told herself as she pulled in and parked beside her brother's truck. Apparently he'd decided to take an early break for dinner before the wave of evening shoppers descended on the shop, leaving his assistant manager on duty. At least she could take comfort in knowing that when he did explode, it wouldn't last for long; he had to get back to work soon. And maybe there was comfort in knowing that she only had to break her news once.

Fingering the slender gold band with her thumb, she slid out of the car. At the same moment Rod emerged from the garage, separate and behind the house. With one look at the hard set of his wide mouth, the remoteness in his eyes, she lost a little of her confidence and shoved her left hand into her coat pocket.

Then she noticed the tools he was carrying to the truck. "What's up? Car trouble?"

"No."

"Oh. Then something must be wrong with the heating system at the nursery because I know you usually do your mechanical work here." She knew she was being uncharacteristically chatty, but that stern expression on his face needed work.

"There's nothing wrong with the heating system."

"The greenhouse pump?"

For a moment he looked as if he was going to ignore her. Then, exasperated, he shut the handful of wrenches and whatnot into the truck's utility box and secured its lock. "I'm doing what you wanted me to do, all right?"

"Excuse me?" Confused and intrigued, Harmony edged closer.

"Paula stopped by the nursery. She ordered a wreath."

"That's nice, Rod, but I don't remember talking to you about selling her one."

He glared at her. "Don't get cute. You know damned well what I mean. You asked me to put her snow tires on for her."

"But you said no," she replied with a shrug.

"Yeah, well..." He exhaled and avoided direct eye contact. "When I saw that she still didn't have them on, I figured if anything happened and she had a wreck, you'd blame me, so I agreed to do it for her later this evening."

Harmony couldn't have been more pleased. As he'd said, she'd had no luck in getting him to help Paula when she'd first asked, even though he knew perfectly well that Paula had no close family left to help her with such things. This convinced her all the more that Rod's feelings for her friend weren't quite as dead as he'd wanted both her and Paula to believe.

"And to think she didn't say a word to me. Wait until I get my hands on her." she cried, clapping her hands together. Laughing, she went to hug her brother. "I'm so glad. Thanks, Rod."

"Don't get any ideas that this means anything."

But although his tone was gruff, there was a hint of a smile on his face. His first in days. Harmony couldn't have been more grateful that he was just talking to her.

"Come on," he grumbled, trying to slip back into old form. "If I'm going to do this, I have to eat and get back to work. I'm running late enough as it is."

Before she could switch sides, he took her left hand. Frowning, he raised it to see what had pricked him. The frown quickly turned into a scowl and he flung away her hand as though she had something contagious.

"What the hell is that?"

This wasn't the way she wanted to break the news to him. They'd given their neighbors enough of a show the night he hit David. She dreaded turning their yard into another theater-in-the-round event. "Can't we go inside? I'll tell all of you about it at the same time."

"You'll tell me now and be quick about it."

Harmony felt her joy slip away as quickly as the sun sinking fast behind the garage. "Rod, please. Don't make a scene."

"Tell me!" he growled.

"I will, but—"

He exploded. "Son of a— It's *him,* isn't it? You told him you'd marry him?"

Knowing the situation would only get worse, Harmony shoved her hands into her pockets and started for the side stairs that led into the kitchen. There was no sense in trying to reason with him when he was like this. He was past listening. She might have inherited their Italian ancestors' passion for music, but he was the one who'd got the fiery Latin temperament. All she could hope for was to get inside before he managed to completely humiliate her. However, she barely got to the third step before he spun her around.

"Answer me when I talk to you!"

The kitchen door burst open and their mother leaned out, her expression horrified. "Rod! What's the matter with you? Have you lost your mind screaming and bellowing like a wounded bear? Come inside before someone thinks heaven knows what and calls the police."

"You'll be yelling, too, in a minute. Wait until you hear what your daughter's done now."

His fury was a physical pressure urging Harmony up the stairs and inside. Not even the wonderful scent of pastries that lingered in the room from her grandmother's day-long holiday baking subdued her concern over what was about to happen.

"What's he talking about?" her mother asked, quickly shutting the door behind them.

Harmony moistened her lips. "We need to talk, Mama."

"Talk?" Rod replied sarcastically. "What's there to talk about? The damage is done. The time to talk was *before* you said yes."

Gran Irena stood by the stove, a wooden stirring spoon in her hand. "Has there not been enough fighting?"

"You'd be surprised," Rod muttered.

Harmony sent her brother a reproachful look, but she remained silent. Instead she used the frighteningly brief interim she knew she had to think of David and pray for the strength and words to make her family understand.

"What are you waiting for?" Rod demanded, ripping down his vest's zipper and jerking it off. "Tell them."

The table was set, and fresh garlic bread was already sitting in a basket in the center of the table, along with equally fresh Parmesan cheese, which meant one of her favorite pasta dishes would be served tonight. She wondered if, once they were finished, anyone would have any appetite to eat.

With her back straight and her head high, she turned, drew her left hand from her coat pocket and held her arm out to her mother and grandmother.

"Madre di Dio!"

"Dear heaven—it can't be!"

Both women's eyes and mouths created perfect circles.

"Harmony, you didn't? Tell us this isn't what it looks like?" her mother whispered through stiff lips.

"It's an engagement ring, Mama," she said, smiling with pride at the clarity of the stone in the well-lit kitchen. "Please be happy for me."

Instead she met only silence. Bowing her head, Harmony lowered her hand and began removing her coat. So be it, she thought.

"Is that the reason you're late this evening?" her mother asked, her voice tinny in the quiet room.

"For the most part."

"You weren't supposed to see him again."

"I never agreed to that, Mama," she replied quietly.

"Knowing how we feel about his family?"

"And while you're asking her *that,* find out how we're supposed to show our faces in town once this gets around," Rod muttered, leaning back against the door and crossing his arms over his chest. "Ask her how she can slap us in the face like that. Ask her how she can give herself to someone carrying the name of her father's murderer."

"Stop it, Rod! That has nothing to do with David. He's a fine, honorable man." Harmony shifted slightly to include her mother and grandmother. "What's more, I told all of you about what David said happened the night Dad died. It was terrible, yes, but it didn't have to happen. Just once you might think about the man who lives, the man whose life is haunted by the knowledge that if Dad had listened to him, he might be with us here today."

Her mother gasped. White-faced, she whispered hoarsely, "Never, *never* say anything like that to me again."

Although her mother's expression shook her, Harmony stood resolute with what she believed, and what was in her heart. "You know me, Mother. You know I've spent my entire life trying to be a good daughter, and you know how much I miss Daddy. But I won't turn my back on life, and that's what you're asking me to do by denying what I feel for David."

She searched her mother's blank eyes, and then her grandmother's. "Mama? Gran? Please. You understand this. We're women. We know about going on."

Her mother stopped twisting her own ring and turned to look out the kitchen window. "If you do this," she said at last, "you'll have no family at your wedding. Do you understand? None."

"But it's Christmas!" Stunned, Harmony spread her arms wide. "If this isn't the season for understanding and empathy, for new beginnings, then what will reach you? What will move you?"

"It won't be this marriage," her mother replied without turning around. "Make your choice, Harmony, by all means. But remember who you are."

Her eyes filling from hurt and pity, Harmony shook her head. "I never thought I would say this, but shame on you, Mama. Your inability to face the truth diminishes you."

David got home just before dawn began to take the sting out of the morning air. He wasn't a bit worn by his long night. Thoughts of Harmony had kept him awake and warm, and he couldn't wait until they could be together again. But first, he thought, drawing a last deep breath of the crisp air, he needed to break his news to his parents.

They were already up and busy in the kitchen. Well, as usual, his father sat at the kitchen table waiting for his plate of goodies. Everyone teased him because breakfast was his favorite meal of the day, and David hoped that was going to work in his favor this morning to influence his mood.

As he entered the kitchen his mother stood at the stove giving a final stir to the eggs that would accompany the hash browns, ham and toast already waiting. The aroma, accented by freshly perking coffee, made his mouth water.

"Morning. Smells great," he said, conscious that neither of his parents smiled or said anything when he entered.

He was being punished for Harmony. He understood that and was even able to accept it, although he rejected its intent. He'd also concluded that the only way to cope was to ignore it. Granted, old ties made it difficult—this was his family, for heaven's sake—but all he had to do was think about Harmony, *Harmony*, and he felt the conviction and blessing of goodness.

"Try to be quiet when you go upstairs. Jolene and Jack got in late last night," his mother announced. "You want your usual breakfast?"

"No, thanks. Just this coffee for now."

As expected, his mother turned to watch him pour. His father even hesitated turning the next page of his paper. "Are you feeling badly this morning?" his mother asked, her expression warming with maternal concern.

"Nope. Feel fine. Great. Finish up there, and come sit down. I'll pour you a cup of coffee, too. Dad, ready for a refill?"

Setting his mug on the table, he quickly shed his jacket and looked expectantly at each parent. The grouping felt good and he hoped Shawna didn't show up earlier than usual—or Jolene and his favorite brother-in-law, for that matter. Not that he had any hesitation about breaking the news to the rest of his family, but he figured if he could convince his mother and father that he was happy and doing the right thing, the rest would be a cinch.

"I'll hold off until the others get down," his mother said.

"I still have a half cup," his father told him. "But what's up?"

Leave it to his old man to cut to the bottom line, David thought, smiling inwardly. "There's something I'd like to share with you. I have a feeling it's going to get around quick and I don't want you to think you weren't the first to know."

His parents exchanged glances. "Sounds serious," his mother said, turning off the stove and spooning the eggs onto his father's plate.

"It is." Taking his seat, David closed his hands around his mug. "I've asked Harmony Martin to marry me. She's accepted."

The only sound that followed was that of the spatula hitting the stove. As it bounced from there to the floor, his father set his paper down on the empty end of the table.

"Is this some kind of a joke?"

"No, sir. Actually, I think asking her to be my wife is the best and smartest thing I've ever done. It's time I settled down and started a family of my own. Past time."

Rising, his mother wiped her hands on her apron. "Well, yes, but... David, you only mentioned going out with her for the first time the other day. Now marriage? This seems rather sudden to me."

"How often did you and Dad go out before he proposed?" David asked, unable to hide a wide grin. The story, much to his parents' chagrin, was brought up with enthusiasm by their children at least three times a year—at each of their birthdays and then their anniversary.

"Your father was going overseas," his mother reminded him, her dignity clearly shot for the morning. "Circumstances were different. We didn't know when we would see each other again."

"Circumstances are always different, Mom. It's called life."

"Don't get smart."

David focused on his father. "Don't treat me like a seventeen-year-old kid, Dad. I've lived at home because I've been happy here. I've respected you. I thought you respected me."

As expected, his father looked away. "Don't go getting stiff-necked. Of course we respect you. You're our only son, for crying out loud. Why do you think we're upset?"

"Oh, you mean if Shawna got engaged to Rod Martin this would be okay?"

The sound of wood scraping across linoleum sounded as his father rose and pushed back his chair. "I'm surrounded by comedians these days," he shouted, gesturing wildly. "My youngest daughter has taken up eating grass and roots so she'll be invisible on stage, my second oldest daughter announces she's pregnant with twins and that she and her husband are opening a *psychic awareness* shop—whatever that is— my eldest daughter tells me that she and her husband are having separate holidays this year because they're *reevaluating* their relationship, and now my son tells me he's engaged to a *Martin?*" His father picked up the butter knife in the middle of the table and offered it to him. "Here. Use this. Believe me, it would be a kindness."

David did take the knife from him, but after setting it back down, he met his father's wild glare calmly. "Why do you wonder where Shawna and Lea got their flair for the dramatic, Dad? You're a born thespian and you don't even know it."

Although his father backed away from him, he pointed determinedly. "Okay, wise guy. Go ahead and laugh. Someday we'll sit down and compare notes and then you can tell me what a joke I am."

"I didn't say that," David said, his humor receding. More than anything, he hated people putting words in his mouth.

Just as quickly his father returned to the table and slapped his palm to the surface. "Her family will never allow it—or will we, for that matter. How could you, David?" he added more softly.

"I love her. That made it easy."

"*Love.*"

As his father burst into laughter, his mother shot him a disapproving look. "Glenn. Don't get too carried away."

They exchanged one of those husband-and-wife looks that outsiders could only speculate about. David didn't pretend to understand. He was only glad his mother seemed to be having an influence.

"Excuse me," his father said, straightening. "I didn't mean to mock what your mother and I share."

"I understand, Dad. Is Lea really pregnant again?" He knew his sister had experienced difficulty conceiving and that she and her husband had been experimenting with other options. As for Toni, she'd always been the aggressive one in the family, the go-getter, and sometimes it had taken too much control of her life. If her husband, Zack, had agreed to this separation, there was a method to the madness.

"Pregnant and expanding," his father replied, sinking back into his chair and shooting him a speaking glance. Then he shook his head. "Son, wake up. Face reality. What your mother and I share is rare. Do you think it's going to be anything like this with Harmony's family cutting at you all the time?"

"Right now the only one cutting is you," David observed gently.

"That's because I'm the only one who sees you're living in a dream world."

"I've never been more awake."

"Uh-uh." His father shook his head. "Because if you were, you'd realize this is going to kill your uncle. And you're going to tell him, I'm not."

David nodded. "That's what I planned. Anything else?"

"Yeah." Once again his father's eyes burned with emotion. "We won't come. We don't approve of this wedding and we won't have any part of it."

David had expected trouble, but nothing this irrefutably close-minded. He glanced at his mother, only to see her turn back to her cooking.

"I've never been ashamed of being a Shepherd," he said, not even trying to hide his disappointment. "Until now."

Chapter Ten

"You want me to be your *what?*"

Harmony stood in the empty corridor of the school and watched tolerantly as Paula took in her news. "My bridesmaid," she explained. "My maid of honor. My witness." She shrugged, because under the circumstances an impromptu, unconventional wedding was difficult to define. "I don't know what to call it, since you and whoever David asks as his witness are bound to be the only ones there besides Father Bernard."

After another few seconds of staring, Paula uttered a whoop and hugged her tight. "You did it. You *did* it! And all these years you kept telling me that I'd be married three times before you tied the knot once."

"Well, there's still a week or so," Harmony replied with an affectionate grin.

"That's pushing things, even for me." But as quickly as she'd cheered, Paula grew somber. "Of course I'll be there. I'd be honored. But what's the matter with your family? Surely they're not going to be pigheaded about this? Never mind," she added when Harmony glanced around, concerned that someone might be within earshot. "I know this isn't the time or place to go into it. But, oh…" She stopped at the hallway intersection that would take them in different directions and hugged Harmony again. "I'm so happy for you."

"Thanks." Harmony beamed. "It means a great deal, believe me."

Paula eyed her closely and nodded. "I can tell you need some cheering up. We can't have our bride-to-be looking less than ecstatic. What are you doing for lunch?"

"I was hoping to spend it with you. I thought we could—you know—plan something."

"Consider it done."

"That would be great. I need all the help I can get. Besides, you owe me an explanation." She shot a sidelong glance at her friend. To Paula's credit Harmony thought she managed to look sincerely perplexed.

"An explanation about what?"

"You and Rod. He didn't mention any of this to you the other night when he changed your tires?"

Despite a smile of apology, Paula shook her head. "Not a peep. But I should have guessed something was up because he was in one foul mood. I just figured it was me."

"No, I inspired that particular black cloud hanging over his head," Harmony replied, remembering the harsh words that had passed between them and the bitterness that had remained. "The question is, what's going to happen for you two? Did he ask you out?"

"No, drat it all. I'm lucky he put the tires back on. All I did was mention how pretty you've been looking these last days, and if that pin you were wearing was a family heirloom or something. Could I help it if I keep forgetting to ask you about it?"

Harmony bit her lower lip, but nodded. "After I showed them my ring and they reacted as though I'd sold government secrets to some unfriendly country, I decided I had nothing to lose. Besides, I'm proud of this pin that David gave me, and annoyed at myself for having hidden it."

Paula nodded and whistled softly. "No wonder your brother got all bent out of shape. For a minute I thought he would leave me parked out in front of the nursery with my car up on those lifts." She sighed, and suddenly gone was her humor and confidence; all that remained was tentativeness. "Maybe it's time to face the fact that Rod and I really are a finished item. I tried to rekindle something new. When you and I talked the other day, I almost began to believe we had a chance, but... He's such a stubborn mule of a man. I can't be this model woman he's created in his mind. I'm me—good, bad and quirky. I told him if he can't handle that, then could we please stop tormenting each other."

Harmony listened. Closely. "*Are* you tormenting each other?"

"Worse than ever." Paula spun away from her, but not before the tears were evident.

"Oh, hon." Harmony didn't care if someone spotted them in the hallway; she embraced her friend. Besides, almost everyone else was supposed to be in classes, and she had a parent-teacher meeting in fifteen minutes, while Paula had a free period. This time was theirs. "I'm so sorry."

Her friend waved off the sympathy and sniffed. "Enough. We'll talk later. *You* concentrate on being happy."

Under these circumstances it was difficult to do so. Aside from the blows she was taking from her family, Harmony grieved for her friend's inability to mend her broken heart. It wasn't until she met David after school to go for their blood tests that she regained the feeling of true bliss that she'd found with him.

"Don't let them get you down, sweetheart," he told her as they sat next to each other in his car outside the doctor's office. He stroked her hand, and she gripped his. "These things have a way of working out."

"I don't know, David. Everyone's either so confused or angry. It's feasible that Rod will throw away his chance for happiness as a result of me, simply because of stubborn pride."

"If he does, it's still his decision to make." He drew her closer for a soothing kiss. "I prefer to think of Christmas Eve."

That immediately brought a change. Harmony smiled.

They'd spoken to Father Bernard after Sunday's service. The priest had been endearingly sympathetic to their plight, and despite an already strained schedule for that special night, he had agreed to perform a brief wedding before the regular candlelight service. Between people like him, Mrs. Silverman and Paula, their future was beginning to take shape.

"A week from Saturday," Harmony murmured. "When I think of how little time there is, I have a panic attack. I haven't figured out when I'm going to go shop for a dress yet!''

"It doesn't matter. You're going to look beautiful no matter what you wear."

She adored him for saying that, but explained how important it was going to be to look special that night and feel confident. "It's *because* we're taking such a big step, and we're doing it virtually alone."

"Then you and Paula go to... New York City on Saturday if you have to, and find whatever you need."

"But we were going to spend the day cleaning and painting the apartment," she felt a need to remind him. "After church on Sunday we were going to start hanging draperies and then bring over some of our things, since I have the concerts during part of next week, and you're working extra hours so you can have a few days off."

"I'll paint myself. It's not going to be as much fun as if you were there," he added, pretending he had a brush and wanted to paint her nose. "But if worse comes to worst, what's the big deal if we move in before everything's perfect? Is that such a problem?"

When put that way, Harmony realized she was worrying about too many small things. "You're right. We shouldn't sweat the small stuff," she murmured, borrowing one of the twins' favorite T-shirt quotes.

That reminded her of what their reaction had been when they'd heard her news. They'd been sweet. Though a bit leery about her marrying a Shepherd, they'd thought their older brother was being "a nerd" for giving her such a hard time.

"Does that mean you won't be taking us skiing anymore?" Brandon had asked with concern.

"Of course it doesn't," she'd assured them. "Nothing will change except that I'll be living in town. In fact, it might even be better. You know David's quite a skier, and I'll bet he could give you a few pointers. Remember how you wanted to learn to slalom, Christopher? At one time David considered trying for the Olympic team."

That had done it for the boys. If only the rest of the family was so easy to deal with.

"This isn't only terrifying, David, it's nerve-racking." She rested her head against his chest as dusk settled about them. One by one the town's streetlights switched on, along with the garland-adorned pole decorations. She focused on the one with the candles that were her favorites.

"Want to change your mind?"

Immediately she sat up. There wasn't a trace of laughter or amusement in his eyes. "No! It's just…at moments like this it hits me that we know so little about each other."

"Says who?" he growled, tugging her against his chest. "I know I love your hair, that you play like an angel, that you have the sexiest mole right under your right breast…."

"David!" Embarrassed as she thought of *that* little detail he'd discovered last night, she tried to squirm away from him, but he would have none of it.

"What I'm trying to say is that the rest is *what* we're supposed to be doing after we're married," he insisted, his expression growing sober. "It isn't knowing that my mother doesn't like war movies and is wild about the color pink that makes my father happy that he's been married to her for thirty-one years. It's knowing that on any given day she might show up on campus with a picnic lunch and even if it's pouring and they have to eat in the car, she's going to make it an adventure he'll be smiling over for days. It's knowing that on his birthday when he would secretly prefer tickets for a ball game in Boston so he can take Douglas, but won't say so because he knows she wants to throw him a party, he'll come home and find the tickets sitting on his bed stand. It's the lifetime of discovery that's going to make us click, sweetheart, and I can't wait."

Harmony knew he needed some reassuring from her, some sense that she understood and agreed, and she slipped her arms around his neck and replied, "I know I'm not the most spontaneous person in the world, but I'd elope tonight if you wanted me to."

He groaned and buried his face in the warm curve of her neck. "Angel eyes, don't say that. You'll make me want to go back inside and demand they rush our certificates so we can hurry up and file for our license."

"At least that would give us a reason not to hope that our families might still show up at our wedding."

He sighed. "They said no, sweetheart. All we can do is tell them when and where. What we mustn't do is let them undermine our happiness."

"You're right. But I can't help dreaming, David."

"Dream of our wedding night," he murmured against her lips before offering her a teasing sample of what she had to look forward to.

But David understood Harmony's dreaming. He dreamed, too.

Convincing her that he could handle getting the apartment ready himself, he sent her off to Burlington on Saturday to shop with Paula. He'd decided after steaming up the car windows and nearly being swept away by the pleasure they found in each other's arms, being alone with her in their future home would be too much temptation. That didn't, however, keep him from fantasizing about how it was going to be.

He was actually grateful when Mrs. Silverman trudged upstairs to bring him a cup of coffee and to see how work was progressing.

"Very nice," she said, circling the sheet-covered room as she eyed the eggshell white walls. "You're going to make me think I'm not charging you enough rent."

"Don't say that," David scolded gently. "This may be a good time to tell you that although Harmony and I would like to wait about a year before we start a family, she wants to save as much as she can for baby furnishings and things."

"I'm only teasing, I'm only teasing. The real reason I'm bothering you is to ask you a technical question about this wedding you want me to participate in. My favorite soap opera just had a wedding, and would you believe they, too, had a woman as best man?"

"So now you know it can be fun."

Although there was a decided twinkle in Mrs. Silverman's eyes, she huffed and grumbled. "Well, fun is fun, but, sweetie, she decided if *she* was going to be a best man, she would wear a tuxedo." The old woman ran her hand over her somewhat bulging middle. "Now, it's interesting enough that I'm participating in a Catholic ceremony, but have you looked at me lately, David, dear? This is not a body you put in a tuxedo."

"Even *I'm* not wearing a tuxedo, Mrs. Silverman," he assured her, saluting her with the steaming mug. "You can wear anything you like—including that pink boa of yours."

"Thank you, darling. That's a relief. As for the boa, I must admit it camouflages my short neck very nicely, but I wouldn't want to outshine the bride. I'll think up something else."

David knew her outfit would probably be unusual no matter what she chose to wear, but he didn't mind. To him, Gladys Silverman seemed to epitomize the spirit of what he and Harmony were seeking—individuality. The right to live their own lives. "Well, I just want you to know that we're grateful you're going to stand up with us. It means a great deal."

"I wouldn't miss it for the world," the old woman gushed. "For once I want to see a Romeo and Juliet story turn out with a happy ending."

"Me, too, Mrs. S. Me, too."

He thought it would take forever for Christmas Eve to arrive. Then suddenly it was the night of the big event. Harmony had moved into the apartment the night before, wanting to avoid any last-minute trauma with her family who'd been treating her as if she was a stranger or guest in the house. David had avoided trouble himself by loading the last of his possessions into his car, then working most of the day. Although the chief knew about his plans, he was honoring David's request to keep it from the rest of the officers until after the wedding. But he'd made sure to send him on his way an hour earlier than David had asked to leave.

When he arrived at Secondhand Treasures he used the extra time to unload his car and store his things in Mrs. Silverman's back room. Since school was already out for the holidays, Harmony was upstairs getting dressed, but Mrs. Silverman resolved the problem of getting ready by offering him the use of her bathroom.

At last, however, while Mrs. Silverman locked up her shop and began changing herself, it was time to go upstairs and see his bride. His heart slamming in his throat, he climbed the stairs, only to discover that she was still sequestered in the bedroom

David paced around the coffee table several times. Then he stood looking out the window where the cheerful lights that Mrs. Silverman had originally hung for them still framed the romantic view of the town lake. Come spring he would take Harmony there for a picnic of their own, he mused. And one day they'd bring their children there to play, learn to swim, and fish.

"David."

He hadn't heard the door open. Turning, he found her standing in the doorway, a tentative smile curving her beautiful mouth.

She looked like a dream in the soft, colorful light, a vision out of some ancient fairy tale. Her dress was a floor-length creation of ivory lace that was modest with its wrist-length sleeves and high collar, except that the slender sheath outlined her slim body like a caress. Instead of a veil, she wore a wreath of baby's breath in her hair—the hair he loved and had begged she wear down. As he'd entreated, it flowed around her shoulders in a bounty of curls, perfect for the romantic look.

"Harmony," he whispered, crossing to her as if in a trance. "You're breathtaking."

"So are you," she replied, her look serene.

He shook his head. His charcoal gray suit was as good as new because he'd worn it only a few times, but even though Shawna insisted it made him look like her favorite movie idol, she made him wish he'd rented that tuxedo after all.

Then she was in his arms and nothing mattered except showing her how much he adored, worshiped her. Their kiss was reverential, but they were both trembling when Mrs. Silverman interrupted them by starting to sing the wedding march downstairs.

"Scared?" he asked, breathing as if he'd run a marathon.

"Excited. This is a dream, David."

"Even though we're virtually alone?"

"We have each other."

He took her hands in his. "Then let's go do it."

Downstairs Mrs. Silverman presented the two of them with her contribution to the event, a red rose and baby's breath boutonniere for him, and a bouquet of miniature gardenias in natural greenery and framed in lace for Harmony.

They both kissed the old woman's lightly rouged cheek and thanked her effusively. They made a great to-do about her attire, too.

"You fox," David teased, taking her hand and carefully coaxing her to do a slow spin.

She wore a matronly suit in a dove gray, perfectly matched to her softly curling hair. No sparkles or flash tonight; her only jewelry was a double string of faux pearls with matching studs at her ears. Even her makeup was toned down. "I feel so naked without my false eyelashes," she confessed, letting David help her on with her black coat. "But I didn't want to give your priest the idea your landlady is a floozy."

"Father Bernard is going to think you're wonderful," Harmony replied, beaming. Then with her on one side of the older woman and David on the other, the three of them started for the church.

"Very nice," Mrs. Silverman offered in a loud whisper as they stood in the narthex of the small cathedral and hung their outer wear on the racks that lined both walls. Harmony smiled and joined the old woman, who stood peeking into the nave of the church.

"I've always loved it best at Christmas," she murmured in agreement.

The stained glass windows along each side of the building seemed to glow with an otherworldliness, thanks to the outside floodlights that were kept lit for night services. The altar and choir sections were adorned with red poinsettias, and candles flickered everywhere.

As Father Bernard emerged from the vestry, they walked down the aisle trimmed with green velvet ribbons to meet him. "Good evening, Father," Harmony murmured, and introduced him to Mrs. Silverman.

"Welcome, welcome," he said, his face aglow with a peace that made him a beloved member of the community. Tonight he was resplendent in white and gold, which made him look something between a less plump Santa Claus and an angel. "You look radiant, my dear," he added to Harmony. "The only disappointment I have tonight is that you won't be singing with the choir or playing for us."

Harmony thought of her own disappointment, and David's, and when she glanced over to him, their eyes met and she knew he understood.

"It looks as if we're ready to begin once the best man arrives," the priest announced.

"That's me, Father," Mrs. Silverman said, raising her hand as though eager to answer a teacher's inquiry.

To his credit he barely blinked. "Charming," he replied with a bow. "Then, Harmony, we're waiting for... Paula, perhaps? I must admit I was surprised when you didn't come in with her."

"Yes, she'll be my attendant, Father. In fact, she should have already been here." Harmony glanced back just as the vestibule doors opened again. "Oh, here she... dear heaven."

Yes, Paula was coming. But she wasn't alone. Following her was Rod, her mother, Gran Irena and the twins, who sent matching grins her way and thumbs-up signals. That's all she could see for several moments after that because her eyes had begun to tear.

"David?"

He was beside her immediately, a steadying arm around her waist. "I don't believe it," he murmured to her.

Paula took Rod's arm and urged the family down the aisle. "Oh, for pity's sake," she grumbled cheerfully, "you're already here. What are you going to do, watch from back there?"

"Paula Carlyle, you have a big mouth," Gran Irena muttered, stony-faced.

To Harmony's added shock her friend only laughed.

"Get used to it, Granny Rina. You may be hearing a lot more of it in the future." Then, after kissing Rod on the cheek and ushering him and the rest of the Martins into a pew on Harmony's side, she joined the group at the altar.

"Is your heart strong enough to take this?" she asked somewhat breathlessly. She looked lovely if a bit windblown in the wine red velvet gown they'd found her at the same little shop where they'd located Harmony's dress.

"I'm not sure," Harmony admitted. "H-how? When?"

"It's a long story. Suffice it to say I wasn't president of my college debating team for nothing. The point *you* should know is that they were half sold on showing up, anyway. They just needed that last push."

"But *Granny Rina?*" Harmony added under her breath, painfully aware that her grandmother despised nicknames.

"Cute, huh? I love the glazed look that gets in her eyes whenever I call her that. And if I can get your brother to defrost the rest of the way, I may get to call her that all the time."

Almost dizzy with shock and happiness, Harmony hugged her friend. "You're the best." Over her shoulder she smiled at her mother and mouthed, "Thank you."

It was a discreet cough from Father Bernard that reminded them they were running on a tight schedule. As if he were a director who loved stage setting, he coaxed them to create a semicircle before him. But just as he drew a breath to speak, another commotion could be heard in the back of the church.

Harmony felt David stiffen. She knew what he must be thinking. Could it be? Did he dare hope? But he didn't take his eyes off Father Bernard. Squeezing his hand because she understood, she was the one to glance back.

Shakily she exhaled and whispered to her husband-to-be, "David, you have to look. Magic."

His fingers bit into hers, but he did as she urged. Coming up the aisle was practically the entire flock of Shepherds—his parents, followed by his sisters and their families. When they reached the Martins, they paused. The two families considered each other, then as though everyone else was holding their breath, Glenn Shepherd nodded.

Maybe it would have been nice if her brother Rod had stood and offered his hand, Harmony thought. But as the heroine of one of her favorite films had succinctly put it, she wasn't one to ask for the moon when they had the stars.

"It has to be magic," David said gruffly as his family took their places in the pews on the opposite side of the aisle. Smiling when they heard his mother whisper, "I need those tissues now, Glenn," he turned back to Father Bernard. "Magic. We're ready now, Father."

"Not magic, children," the priest replied with a beautiful smile. "Miracles. This is the night for them." Then he said more loudly, "Shall we begin . . . ?"

Epilogue

"David, you'll fall. We'll *both* fall."

"Oh, ye of little faith." He even managed to kiss his wife as he topped the last few steps to their apartment. "Home sweet home," he announced as he nudged the door shut with his foot.

Home...with his wife. It felt so good David still couldn't believe it was true.

The service had been brief, as Father Bernard had warned, but memorable. The entire night had been memorable, thanks to their families.

"I still can't believe they all came," Harmony said, as though reading his mind.

She was right. Oh, there was a critical moment once again as Father Bernard pronounced them man and wife and their families swarmed them to offer their congratulations. Shepherds and Martins inevitably came face-to-face. It was Mrs. Silverman who saved the day and put it all in perspective.

"Hey, people!" she'd announced in the stiff silence. "If I can be here and be happy for these dear kids, then you can find it in your heart to share their joy."

"Did your family ever say what convinced them to come?" Harmony asked him. "I tried to listen for some explanation, but that impromptu reception they threw us after the candlelight service was incredibly noisy."

David shrugged. "Only that they realized in the last week, with me being gone so much, that this was how their life was going to be without me. But I am sorry your family turned down the invitation to join us."

"Me, too. But we'll stop by tomorrow as we promised. It'll be easier for them to do things slowly. Besides, it was a big move for my grandmother to invite Mrs. Silverman to spend the night at their place so we would have privacy," she added, stroking his cheek.

Invited? David smiled. Harmony's grandmother had *insisted* his best man stay in Harmony's old room so he and Harmony could enjoy complete privacy for their first night of marriage. "She won my heart," David said, completing his trek to their bedroom.

Although the room was unlit, there was enough light coming through the windows from the decorations in town to let him admire his beautiful bride as he lowered her to their bed. He followed, relishing the pleasure of feeling her body against his.

"I love you," he said, not for the first time that night. He'd been holding off saying it. Even when he'd asked her to marry him, he'd resisted letting it spill from him. Harmony had admitted tonight that she'd thought it a bit odd, but had thought that perhaps he was just one of those people who had difficulty saying those three little words. Not the case. He'd promised himself that he wouldn't say it until she was truly, totally his. And he hadn't stopped since.

"I love you," Harmony replied, looping her arms around his neck. She drew him down so they were completely touching from lips to feet. In fact, when David kicked off his shoes, he used his toes to nudge off hers. She laughed with delight. "That feels wonderfully decadent."

He loved seeing her literally shimmer with happiness. He loved knowing that they needn't hurry to satisfy the hunger that kept bringing secret smiles to their eyes whenever their gazes met. He loved *her*, with all his heart.

"This is the best Christmas present I'll ever have," he murmured, sliding his arms under her to bring her closer yet.

"We'll see about that," she teased softly.

And in her smile he saw all the Christmases in their future... the ones he knew would be filled with new life, love and family. It was the last thing he needed to see before closing his eyes and offering his wife his soul.

*   *   *   *   *

Another wonderful year of romance
concludes with

Christmas Memories

Share in the magic and memories of romance
during the holiday season with this collection of two
full-length contemporary Christmas stories,
by two bestselling authors

**Diana Palmer
Marilyn Pappano**

Available in December at your favorite retail outlet.

MILLION DOLLAR SWEEPSTAKES (III)

presents

WATCHING FOR WILLA
by Helen R. Myers

Willa's new neighbor was watching her.
Her every move, her every breath. With his
mysterious past, Zachary Denton was an
enigma. He claimed he only wanted to
warn her, protect her—possess her. And
like a butterfly drawn into a deadly web,
Willa could not resist his mesmerizing
sensual pull.

But was he a loving protector—or a
scheming predator?

Find out this February—only from
Silhouette Shadows.

MONTANA Mavericks

Stories that capture living and loving
beneath the Big Sky, where legends live
on...and mystery lingers.

This December, explore more MONTANA MAVERICKS with

THE RANCHER TAKES A WIFE
by Jackie Merritt

He'd made up his mind. He'd loved her almost a lifetime
and now he was going to have her, come hell or high
water.

And don't miss a minute of the loving as the passion con-
tinues with:

> **OUTLAW LOVERS**
> by Pat Warren (January)
>
> **WAY OF THE WOLF**
> by Rebecca Daniels (February)
>
> **THE LAW IS NO LADY**
> by Helen R. Myers (March)
> and many more!

Only from **Silhouette®** where passion lives.

Is the future what it's cracked up to be?

This December, discover what commitment
is all about in

GETTING ATTACHED: CJ
by Wendy Corsi Staub

C. J. Clarke was tired of lugging her toothbrush
around town, and she sure didn't believe longtime
boyfriend David Griffin's constant whining about
"not being able to commit." He was with her every
day—and most nights—so what was his problem?
C.J. knew marriage wasn't always what it was cracked
up to be, but when you're in love you're supposed to
end up happily ever after…aren't you?

The ups and downs of life as you know it continue with

GETTING A LIFE: MARISSA
by Kathryn Jensen (January)

GETTING OUT: EMILY
by ArLynn Presser (February)

Get smart. Get into "The Loop"!

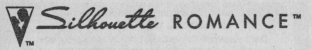

SILHOUETTE... Where Passion Lives

Don't miss these Silhouette favorites by some of our most
distinguished authors! And now you can receive a discount by
ordering two or more titles!

SD#05786	QUICKSAND by Jennifer Greene	$2.89	☐
SD#05795	DEREK by Leslie Guccione	$2.99	☐
SD#05818	NOT JUST ANOTHER PERFECT WIFE		
	by Robin Elliott	$2.99	☐
IM#07505	HELL ON WHEELS by Naomi Horton	$3.50	☐
IM#07514	FIRE ON THE MOUNTAIN		
	by Marion Smith Collins	$3.50	☐
IM#07559	KEEPER by Patricia Gardner Evans	$3.50	☐
SSE#09879	LOVING AND GIVING by Gina Ferris	$3.50	☐
SSE#09892	BABY IN THE MIDDLE	$3.50 u.s.	☐
	by Marie Ferrarella	$3.99 can.	☐
SSE#09902	SEDUCED BY INNOCENCE	$3.50 u.s.	☐
	by Lucy Gordon	$3.99 can.	☐
SR#08952	INSTANT FATHER by Lucy Gordon	$2.75	☐
SR#08984	AUNT CONNIE'S WEDDING		
	by Marie Ferrarella	$2.75	☐
SR#08990	JILTED by Joleen Daniels	$2.75	☐

(limited quantities available on certain titles)

AMOUNT	$_____
DEDUCT: 10% DISCOUNT FOR 2+ BOOKS	$_____
POSTAGE & HANDLING	$_____
($1.00 for one book, 50¢ for each additional)	
APPLICABLE TAXES*	$_____
TOTAL PAYABLE	$_____
(check or money order—please do not send cash)	

To order, complete this form and send it, along with a check or money order
for the total above, payable to Silhouette Books, to: In the U.S.: 3010 Walden
Avenue, P.O. Box 9077, Buffalo, NY 14269-9077; In Canada: P.O. Box 636,
Fort Erie, Ontario, L2A 5X3.

Name:_____

Address:_____ City:_____

State/Prov.:_____ Zip/Postal Code:_____

*New York residents remit applicable sales taxes.
Canadian residents remit applicable GST and provincial taxes.   SBACK-DF

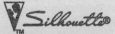